I0583945

Metaphorosis

June 2020

Beautifully made speculative fiction

Also from Metaphorosis

Verdage

Reading 5X5 x2: Duets
Score – an SFF symphony
Reading 5X5: Readers' Edition
Reading 5X5: Writers' Edition

Metaphorosis Magazine

Metaphorosis: Best of 20xx
Metaphorosis 20xx: The Complete Stories
annual issues, from 2016

Monthly issues

Plant Based Press

Best Vegan Science Fiction & Fantasy
annual issues, from 2016

from B. Morris Allen:
Susurrus
Allenthology: Volume I
Tocsin: and other stories
Start with Stones: collected stories
Metaphorosis: a collection of stories

Metaphorosis

June 2020

edited by
B. Morris Allen

ISSN: 2573-136X (online)
ISBN: 978-1-64076-171-1 (e-book)
ISBN: 978-1-64076-172-8 (paperback)

Metaphorosis
a magazine of speculative fiction
from
Metaphorosis Publishing

Neskowin

June 2020

The Record Collector

Nathaniel Williams

The first time the house yells at them, it sounds like her husband. Eileen Ulmstead-Barris springs up in bed and looks at Preston lying next to her, motionless in his favored sleeping position —on his back, with his head buried under a pillow that should have smothered any sounds rising from his mouth. The shouts become louder and louder, then stop. Moments later, another cry fills the room.

He must be having an awful nightmare, she thinks. When he is awake, Preston rarely raises his voice for anything. Eileen, half-asleep, shifts the duvet atop her, reaches for the pillow, and pulls it from

Preston's face. He looks peaceful, eyes shut, bathed in the green light of the digital alarm clock.

More shouts follow. Preston's voice is echoing across the walls.

But his lips aren't moving.

Why isn't he waking up? She stops herself from nudging him, reminded of warnings she's heard about not waking a dreamer. Or is that a sleepwalker? She hesitates until a piercing shriek rings out and Preston shifts in his sleep and speaks to her.

"Eileen," he mutters as he rolls over, his back now to her, "turn off your damn alarm."

Years later, Preston Barris will feel compelled to explain his comment from that first night—"Eileen does that a lot. Hits 'snooze' in the morning a dozen times before she gets out of bed. She's a hard sleeper, and not exactly considerate of the person next to her. I just heard noises and assumed it was her clock going off."

The next night, he isn't so lucky. The shouts sound like Eileen, and they both sit awake until morning.

All this happened over a decade ago. Remember that time? Before the housing bubble burst? Homes appreciated in exponents associated with Vegas slot machines or near-mint Silver Age comic books. Everyone—from retirees to new college grads like Eileen and Preston—was urged to get in on it.

Hindsight is never 20/20. It's purblind and tainted by the present's dominating hues. In truth, most of us ignore bad omens in times of plenty, and what we think of as the good old days never seem that great as we live through them. What happened to Eileen and Preston screams "Bad Omen" to anyone willing to believe it. Questions will go unanswered, morals will be left cloudy, as their story proceeds. It's not an urban legend or *This American Life* podcast. The house didn't have seven gables or gingerbread sweets beckoning its purchasers inside. It was just a mock Tudor in St. Louis, Missouri, an upscale, milquetoast neighborhood in fly-over country.

Things get weirder. Eileen and Preston talk things over. (They talk everything over. Preston insists on consensus decision-making.) They review the details.

She wants to hire a plumber just in case it's something in the pipes. He wants to banish whatever spectre has obviously invaded their home.

See, Preston's a magician. Not the kind who does card tricks or saws ladies in half onstage. He's a wizard. Or warlock. Eileen isn't sure which he prefers and, truth be told, he changes it on her. She's heard people call the stuff he does Wicca, although he shuns that term and says his rituals are completely different. It mostly involved him building a small worship space in an armoire—filled with candles, incenses, and trinkets that looked like an antique jewelry store display—and sitting in front of it irregularly, an act with all the outward appearances of daydreaming. On specific nights of the year, he meets a group of friends somewhere and they'll daydream together. It's not Eileen's thing, but she gets it.

In the end, they just can't blow a hundred bucks or more on a plumber. At least not while she's working at that rinky-dink radio station. (Maybe Preston doesn't say the last bit aloud, but she knows he thinks it.)

Eileen runs programming at the local public FM station. The volunteer deejays think Eileen is yuppie scum infiltrating their cool, community radio scene. Only she and the General Manager actually get salaries. She also gets a battleship grey credenza in the corner of the entry room. She doles out the shifts. She generates the programming logs that go to the FCC. When something breaks, she explains why they can't fix it. Every day, something breaks.

Deejays come in to her office, demanding new headphones, better mics, shinier toggle switches on the control board.

No, she says.

She knows the budget, they don't. It doesn't matter. She still feels like a fraud.

Every now and then, someone sneers at her, something like "Oh, that's right, you're the music programming director who *doesn't even like music!*"

"*That's me*," she says flatly, but feels her face reddening as she goes back to running things.

The only deejay who talks to her like a person is Len, a retired St. Louis county firefighter, father of four, grandpa of nine, who plays jazz on Thursday afternoons but comes in daily and makes a pot of coffee for everyone. He's a good listener, and Eileen confides in him.

"So, Preston thinks the house is..." Len asks.

"Yeah," she says. "But he's sort of into the freaky stuff." Preston would die if he heard her put it that way. "He's more willing to accept the... supernatural."

"Well," Len says, "Such things aren't unheard of around here, you know."

He means *The Exorcist*. Supposedly, the events that take place in the book and movie are based on something that really happened in St. Louis back in 1949. Sure, they'll tell you, the movie is set outside Washington, D.C., and that's where the actual possessed child was discovered. But the exorcism itself? That happened downtown in the old Alexian Brothers Hospital on Osage Street, just a few blocks off fabled Route 66. You can't bring up anything supernatural in that town without someone mentioning it, as if they've been waiting the whole conversation for the chance. They're like Texans with the Alamo.

"You know who's into that kind of thing? Retro Roddy. The guy who does Saturdays. Have you talked to him?"

"No. Preston's already got a friend coming by to give the place a once-over."

"Hmm." Len says, sipping his coffee. "A supernatural once-over."

The house isn't them. That's the problem.

Couples less than five years out of college don't own homes in Webster Groves. These old Tudor houses with brick and ivy and vaulted wooden doors straight out of Sherwood Forrest, the curving sidewalks lined with boxwood and towering sycamores—they belong to the older St. Louis-area residents. Lawyers, pediatricians, aerospace engineers. The guy who's an advertising agency VP. The gal who owns a chain of organic grocery stores. They deserve these houses. Not Eileen and Preston. Not yet.

But they could afford the house, despite its coveted location. They're both only children of well-situated parents. Preston's folks had him late, died young, and left an inheritance, and Eileen's parents gave her a smaller chunk of cash when they moved to Phoenix, and still call regularly to remind her of their largess.

Their regular phone call comes during the aforementioned Supernatural Once Over, as Preston pours herbal tea for a pretty woman. His friend Greta is skinny, perky, and prone to halter-tops, sheer batik skirts, and mounds of bone-and-turquoise jewelry.

"We have to soothe it," Greta tells them. "You don't give orders to powers like this. Once it feels relaxed, the creepy stuff will stop."

Greta explains how they should temporarily treat whatever-it-is like a roommate, someone who has as much right to live there as them. Then she begins talking about her current live-in boyfriend, who recently stiffed her for two months' rent.

Eileen feels some relief when the phone rings.

"So, how's our Eileen?" her father says.

"Okay."

"Still stressed out at work?"

"Yes."

"And Preston?"

"We're okay," she says.

"Just okay?"

"Yes, Dad. Last I checked 'okay' means nothing's wrong. Did someone change that without telling me?"

"I can just hear it in your voice. You don't sound happy."

Happy.

Her parents put a high value on happy. When she was a child, the two of them stayed happy by smoking copious amounts of marijuana on the couch while she made them peanut butter sandwiches. They weren't complete burnouts, but they didn't have long-term goals until Eileen hit middle school. Suddenly, they worked more nights and weekends. Dad got promoted to head of maintenance for several commercial office buildings. Mom got her real estate license. They transformed.

Weeks later, Preston and Greta are neck deep in talking to the house, but the house keeps shouting. They light candles that smell like burnt hair and cinnamon. Eileen can't help but question if this aromatherapy is what the house really needs. She holds back from speaking the thought that never leaves her mind—*Are you sure you know what you're doing?*

Then, one night she arrives home early hoping to get a nap and finds Greta alone in the house running the vacuum cleaner over little piles of salt sprinkled all around the carpet. Apparently, Greta now has a key. Greta has a milk crate full of toiletries and an overflowing rucksack by the door. Greta herself oozes gratitude for Eileen and, especially, Preston.

"You've got yourself quite a guy there, Eileen Barris," she says. "You're a lucky gal."

"Thank you," Eileen replies automatically.

That night, Eileen tries to understand.

"Greta jumped the gun. I told her that you and I would talk about it," Preston says. "But, look, this thing is taking a lot of time. Greta says maybe weeks. She's on the outs with her roommate, and it makes sense for her to stay with us."

"Things are crazy enough around here."

"She's doing a lot of work—unpaid, mind you—and here's a nice way to thank her."

"I'm not sure."

"Well, she needs to be here. You don't understand how these things work."

Eileen understands that Greta is broke, has been kicked to the curb by her boyfriend, and now has a free place to crash for a few weeks.

Before she can protest, several gunshot-like pops come from the kitchen. A pool of red covers the linoleum. Eileen traces the liquid up the side of the counter, where six shattered bottles of Cabernet Sauvignon sit in the wine rack.

Then the laughter starts. It is a sarcastic, staccato tittering punctuated by snorts.

"That's your laugh," Preston says, backing away from the spill and out the kitchen door. "And that was *my* wine."

It is. Their house is laughing at her with her own voice.

She gets a mop and a bucket and starts to clean.

Eileen leaves for work the next morning without waking Greta, who is immobile on the couch, and without talking to Preston, who will, she knows, take this as her tacit approval of his plan.

The next day, she searches Human Resources files for Retro Roddy's number and—upon discovering only an empty Manila folder—asks Len to help contact him.

Retro Roddy agrees to meet her at Uncle Bill's Pancake and Dinner House, off Kingshighway Blvd. He shows up late. Eileen takes a syrup-sticky booth in the back, near the window facing the parking lot, a long path of corners, wooden beams, and ugly carpet between her and the other patrons.

Although he has effectively been her employee for two years, Eileen has never met Retro Roddy. He deejays midnight to 2 a.m. on Saturdays and skips all organizational meetings, but always submits the mandatory log sheet of songs he played, handwritten in red, felt-tip ink with letters so crisp and legible they'd make a typewriter envious. These lists mean nothing to Eileen. As long as the songs are free of profanity, as long as they garner a listenership, and as long as those listeners free their bank accounts of discretionary income during pledge drives —and they do, Roddy has a following—she doesn't care what he plays.

Although he's a stranger, she knows him instantly. A faded red vintage automobile—a 1965 Ford Falcon, she later learns—pulls into the parking lot, taking up two spaces. A man stumbles out, the bangs of his gray-tinged mop-top spilling over the edges of his Wayfarers. The black t-shirt under his red velvet sports coat is a size too tight and reveals the thinnest white line of beer belly where it rises over his even tighter striped pants. His shoes are snakeskin, narrowed to Keebler-elf points at the tip.

"Smokin' section!" he bellows when he sees her, nodding to the other side of the restaurant, the one filled to capacity.

Eileen relinquishes her privacy, joins him at a smoking booth, and tells her story. Roddy waves his Lucky Strike like an orchestra conductor as she talks. He fiddles with packet after packet of sugar. Some even get poured into his coffee.

"Well, *amiga*," he says, "what I can't do is tell you why it's happening, if you're cursed or unlucky or paying for crimes of your past or someone else's. Give that up. If you need that, I'm not your man. What I *can* do, is get rid of it with a little time and some money."

The figure he asks for is low. Very low. She agrees instantly.

"I get paid when you get your house back. First, I need to come by your place and have a look around. Will it get ugly?"

"No," she says, "Preston and Greta are pretty reasonable. Just stubborn."

"I meant the house. Is it throwing stuff off the shelves? Slinging cutlery or plates around? Is there any gunk or goo dripping? Any bloooood?"

"No."

"Don't worry about your guy and the witch. They're fellow travelers, so to speak. We may do things differently, but we should see eye to eye. I can be diplomatic as hell when I need to be."

That night, she gets to see Roddy's brand of diplomacy firsthand. As anticipated, Greta and Preston feel slighted, even betrayed, that she has brought him. Beads of sweat form on Eileen's temples, doubts made tangible by the Midwestern humidity.

"Here's how it works," Roddy explains. "I set up my stuff and see if the house responds. When I get a sign, we'll all know. Then I'll be able to tell if this will take days or weeks."

Eileen clenches her teeth in a wave of despair—*weeks?*—but Roddy doesn't pause for questions.

"I need until 10 o'clock tonight to test things. After that, you can decide if you want to see this thing through. If it don't work, you never need to see me again."

It is apparently the right thing to say. They agree he'll leave by ten p.m.

"Okay," he says. "Let's hit it!"

He steps back, crosses his legs and spins around on his heel, like something from a Four Tops routine.

Over his shoulder, he shouts "Anyone want to help me fetch my stuff out of old horse?"

"Horse?" Greta says.

Only Eileen follows him out.

By the time she reaches his Ford, he has retrieved what looks like a battered suitcase from his back seat. He stands before her with a stoic frown, something like a gunslinger holding his Peacemaker. But then memories of the area's favorite horror flick arise, and Eileen pictures old Max Von Sydow in the movie poster, with his suitcase, hat, and trench coat, standing outside, that house that creepy light shining down from little Regan's window. Darn Len and his St. Louis folklore.

Roddy opens the car's trunk, which holds a tangle of red and white wires and some electronics equipment, and many,

many wooden crates filled with old records.

"Grab an armload," he says.

Eileen remembers her father crouched near the living room floor, rubbing his chin, as he tested his hi-fi system. Fiddling with speaker wire. Turning knobs. Moving speakers inches to the left or right.

When she got older, she chalked up her father's pursuit of what he called "Optimum Sound" to mild stoner paranoia, figuring the subtle differences in aural quality were figments of his marijuana-laced imagination.

Yet, here's Roddy doing the exact same thing in her living room.

He makes patterns on the ground, geometric shapes of speaker cable, twirling them like a lasso as they fall onto the carpet. The cords all feed into his amplifier, rivers emptying into a Mississippi delta, flowing directly to the New Orleans basin that is Roddy's record player, which looks handcrafted from many other machines.

Eileen winces, recalling her father's eccentricities and realizes she's already invested too much into Roddy. She needs him to succeed. She feels Preston and Greta's growing contempt as they watch Roddy twirl and backstep.

He begins to play the music.

"Now it's gotta be loud, you understand," Roddy shouts over the song.

He sits down on the couch, puts his shoes on the coffee table, and shushes Preston when he tries to speak. For hours, Roddy plays an array of things. One record is old blues music with clicks and scratches, the next is a pristine-sounding rock record with violins and French horns. Sometimes he plays just one song, other times a whole album side. By the end of the night, album covers litter their floor.

Sometimes Greta covers her ears or furrows her brow, frustrated by the strange sounds, until Roddy plays a piano solo.

"That's 'Clair de Lune,'" she says, shocked to recognize something.

"Yeah, Debussy's occultism is well documented. I'm pretty sure he composed it for just this kinda thing."

As the music ends, the house begins to vibrate.

"*Moooooooore. More, pleassse,*" it croons.

Roddy rushes to switch the record to a 45 single.

"Don't change it if that's what it wants!" Greta says.

"That ain't how it works. Just listen."

They hear violins and a chorus of oohs and aahs.

" 'Since I Don't Have You' by the Skyliners," Roddy whispers proudly as the house stops jiggling. "Works like a charm. It's basically 'Clair de Lune,' but with more teenager."

The house sits quiet and still.

Roddy nods. "OK. Here's how it works," he says. "This song's just enough different from the one I played before it to make the Whatever-It-Is in your house uncomfortable without makin' it *mad*. We gotta convince it to move on by changing the music. *Gradually.* We can't just throw music it hates at it all of a sudden. Just over time play crazier stuff. Harder stuff. Spiritual stuff."

Crazy, hard, and spiritual, Eileen thinks. *Sure. Why not?* She has grown tired of waiting for Greta and Preston to get results.

"C'mere and take a look." He motions them towards the record player. "We're gonna keep this song playin' for the rest of the night. The song will replay when it finishes as long as this here lever stays put. Do *not* touch the lever. And let it keep going when you leave for work. I'll come by tomorrow, bring more records, and we'll see if we can stop it once and for all."

"So we're supposed to sleep while the song repeats?" Preston says.

"Well, yeah. It's pretty mellow. Be glad the house didn't respond to speed metal or something."

A Spanish dancer exposes her bare breasts in a sepia photograph.

Two businessmen shake hands as one of them ignites into flames.

Four men inside a large television set run from an enormous cartoon space villain.

A shaggy dog-thing jumps a racing hurdle.

These are but a few covers in Roddy's record collection, strewn out like an illusionist's deck of cards across her living room carpet. To her surprise, Eileen recognizes some faces—Prince astride his purple motorcycle, Springsteen leaning on his Cadillac convertible.

Preston is at work. Greta is elsewhere. Roddy will be back soon. Alone inside her strangely-behaving house, still in work clothes, Eileen has only one thought—

I should be more scared.

But she'd been scared before. Managing a station full of radio renegades who see right through her "by-the-book" façade—that is scary. Her last semester of college, facing graduation alone, searching for a first job alone, before she met Preston—that was scary. Raising herself, arranging rides to Girl Scouts and schedules for her homework due dates, while her Mom and Dad played parental hooky—that was scary.

She hears Roddy's Falcon pull up and goes to meet him. He wears a jean jacket covered with buttons with band names, a wide-lapelled paisley shirt, and bell-bottoms.

"Need help unloading your trusty horse?" she asks.

"Did you say *horse*?" he says. "Like Trigger or Silver? You misheard me." He shakes his head and runs his palm across the car's bumper. "His name's *Horus*. Like the Egyptian sky god, son of Osiris. Some of those designers at Ford knew what they were doin' back in the 60's. Same thing Hitler's bozos did with the scarab back when they designed the Volkswagen." He slaps the car's hood. "This here is two tons of rolling V8 talisman. No black magic in the world that can contend with this."

Inside, he examines several records like a Japanese gardener pruning a bonsai tree, head tilting, nose an inch away from grooves. "So you're not into the witchcraft stuff like your husband?" he asks, barely looking up.

"No. I'm not anything."

"Unaffiliated?"

"Yeah."

"I've known a few guys who practiced the old craft. Most of 'em were in covens. Said it really got them in touch with their feminine side. Sounded like they spent a lot of time standing around naked watching candles burn."

"I don't think his worship is like that," Eileen says.

All the things she doesn't know about Preston's beliefs, his other world. The gaps in her knowledge are immense.

Roddy raises his palms defensively. "Hey, I'm not belittling his faith. I just do things kinda different. Hell, I was raised by heavy duty born-again Christians. *Way* weirder than any pagan-types I ever met." Roddy took a sip of beer and gestured at the jumble on the floor. "They weren't too happy when I took to rock 'n' roll. Called it the Devil's music. But, hey, sometimes you can't control what speaks to you, y'know?"

Neighbors watch the blood red car coming and going each afternoon, just as they had seen the wispy woman in flowing dresses moving in, one cardboard box at a time.

A few neighborhood dignitaries stop by one night to make sure they aren't prepping to sell the place.

Where else would you want to go?

This is a great place to raise kids, when you're ready, of course.

People here look out for one another.

If you ever are tempted to sell, please be sure to start well above appraised value.

Many assume it's a *ménage a quatre*, just another case of suburban polygamy springing up. But who's buggering whom?

The neighbors aren't the only curious ones.

Eileen's mother calls one night while Roddy is playing records. All goes fine until her mother asks to say hello to Preston.

"He's not home yet."

"But I heard music in the background. Are *you* listening to...?"

"No," Eileen says. "We have a guest. A guy from work."

"While Preston's gone? Oh, honey...."

"It's not what you think."

"You know, if it *was*, I'd never tell Preston."

"No. Mom. How could that possibly be okay with you?"

"I just want whatever's best for you. I can sense that you're unhappy. Your father says he hears it in your voice, but you never share details. Talk to me."

A tiny earthquake ripples across the floor, shaking a stack of coasters from the coffee table. The music has stopped.

The armoire filled with Preston's talismans and charms tilts on the wall, its door swinging forth and dumping all its contents onto the floor. Not good.

Eileen groans, too exhausted to panic. "I have to go, Mom."

"My bad," Roddy says. "I'll pick 'em up and put 'em back."

"No," she almost shouts.

As she begins gathering talismans, she realizes that, even if none of them are broken, there is *no way* she can put them back exactly as Preston had them. He'll know. And that means she'll have to tell him this happened. And he'll be petulant and smug.

Eileen watches Roddy hunched and frantic, turning EQ knobs ever so slightly this way or that. Roddy is *not* the kind of man Eileen could ever see herself leaving Preston for. Too much like her dad.

And she knows that ultimately Preston is more likely to leave *her*. She's avoided thinking about what could have happened between him and Greta while she was gone. The thought of Preston alone with another woman doesn't make her paranoid. Their sex life stalled a while back, but that's just how a marriage works sometimes. Right? His inattention. Her disinterest. It is hard to separate the two. Maybe Greta is satisfying him, and that explains it. Or maybe Roddy is right about magic getting Preston in touch with his "feminine side" and he will out himself in a few weeks or months or years and leave her for another guy. She can't guess. The lack of emotion chills her.

Then, that night, Roddy leaves some old love song on replay—full of sad, majestic echoes. Even though she knows these sounds are probably just recording studio tricks, something about hearing it at that moment sends a fissure through her soul. She cries herself to sleep.

"I can't handle this," Greta says, hoisting an armload of dirty clothes on top of her sleeping bag and peering over the stack at Eileen. "Your friend is nuts. And his music stinks."

Eileen, just back from work, watches Greta sashay down the sidewalk toward her car. She has to find out what happened before Preston gets home. Her story needs to be straight.

Roddy shouts over the music, which is indeed louder and faster than the previous evening. Today, he wears a powder-blue Nehru jacket with matching polyester slacks and white Converse.

"She's just pissed 'cause this is *workin'*, man. C'mon. You *knew* she'd have a fit like this, didn't you?"

Eileen doesn't answer.

"And I'm bettin' you aren't sorry to see her go."

True enough.

Roddy takes another sip of beer. At least he brings his own food and drink, which is more than could be said of Greta. Unlike her, Roddy leaves the space in shambles while tallying impeccably printed "billable hours" in a spiral notebook he keeps in his pocket. That's a hundred times more forthright than Greta, who re-enters and checks under tables and behind doors, determined not to leave anything behind.

Preston enters. "Why's your stuff out in the street?" he asks Greta.

"I'm sick of his music!" She points at Roddy.

Preston strides across the room and turns off the stereo, like a TV cop deliberately locking the interrogation room door behind him to intimidate a felon. Eileen knows this move. *He's going to sound rational, but he just wants to get his way.* This will not end well.

Eileen can't think. Her head feels like it could split open. She hears something ripping.

Across the room, Preston's brown leather sofa begins shedding its skin like a snake. Each cushion spontaneously tears and vomits forth beige stuffing. They hear a disembodied voice—clearly Eileen's— laughing maniacally.

Preston points to the deflated sofa. "You wrecked my altar, now my couch. This... this can't happen again."

"It won't if we keep the music goin', man. That was *your* bad, turnin' off the stereo halfway through a song. How many times did I warn you?"

Roddy turns back to his record player. The music starts again, loud and angry.

"I vote we all go out for margaritas while Roddy packs up his stuff," says Greta.

"Aye," says Preston.

"He stays," Eileen tells them. She begins picking up chunks of stuffing from the floor as Preston and Greta storm out.

Right then, Eileen understands two things.

1) Preston is upset because all this has hit him personally—his wine bottles, his sofa, his altar.

2) Everything in the house is *his* or *theirs*. She would never feel as upset as Preston because there is nothing of hers for the Whatever-It-Is to destroy. Nothing belongs to her. She just cleans up the mess when something breaks.

Then, she is just mad. Mad at a husband who cares more about a sofa and candles than he does about her. Mad at her ex-stoner parents who don't care whether her marriage succeeds or fails. Mad at the whole damn city of St. Louis for being so weird.

The song that plays has some English guy yelping behind a wall of guitars. He sounds like he's trying to bite off his tongue as he sings. He says he wants a "ride home."

Me too, she thinks. But she is home.

"I want a ride," she sings. "I want a ride. A ride home."

"Not *ride*." Roddy says. "*Riot*. 'White Riot,' man. You never heard the Clash? You really don't know beans about music do you?"

That evening, he gives her a quick primer on musicians he loves. People with names like Sky Saxon, Black Francis, Exene, and Esquerita.

"These guys were badass," he says. He raises a yellow album labelled "Bad Brains". Its cover shows the U.S. Capitol dome being struck by lightning and cracking down the center like Humpty Dumpty's shell. On the back cover, there is a picture of four black men with dreadlocks.

"Rastafarians," he says. "Freakin' rastas playing hardcore. That's like, I dunno, a bunch of Mormons spinning whirling dervishes. That's *real* magic, man."

Her parents once told her that Rastas based their religion around pot. Well, Rastas believe in something. Like Preston believes in something. Like Roddy and her father believe in something. She's spent her entire life standing next to believers, making silent excuses for their peculiarities. Where did that leave her? Unmoored. Unanchored. A human shell. Could some belief temper the swirling loneliness that fills her lungs and churns in her stomach? If wanting could make belief happen, she'd have it right now, but the moment passes and she knows that no amount of magic, weed, tears, or electronics equipment can fill her.

Preston doesn't return that night. Eileen falls asleep to the sound of Rastas playing hardcore and wakes in the morning to find Roddy still on watch near the record player, sitting with his head inches away from the speaker.

When Eileen returns home that night, Preston is emptying dresser drawers into boxes. Most of the kitchen utensils are packed. More empty boxes wait.

"I want to protect my stuff. You're listening to a mental case instead of me." His voice never wavers. "And he's taking forever."

"*Your* way was taking forever," she says.

He shakes his head like he's ashamed for her. "It's time to take care of what's mine."

"That sounds like Greta's advice," she says. *Or my mother's*, she thinks. "So you're moving out?"

"I don't want to discuss that yet, Eileen."

"Well... I do. Is this the end?"

"If you make me to choose now, you may not like my decision."

Music swells downstairs, where Roddy stands guard. Guitars roar. Snare drums pop like firecrackers.

"I think you've already decided," she says. "You just won't admit it to yourself. You want to think it's all my decision so it's easier on you."

He heads down the hall before she finishes.

Roddy flinches a little as Preston slams the door. He stands with an opened beer, wearing a lime green car coat and a black velvet shirt with airplane-wing lapels.

"Is he the kind that comes back in a day or two after he cools?" Roddy asks. "Or the kind that has his lawyer call you next month?"

"I don't know. He's never left me before."

She could do a million things with this moment—go after Preston, throw Roddy out, go for a long walk to clear her head.

Instead, she turns off the record player. The floor begins to tremble instantly.

"You said something about pushing it out gradually. What if we played something that pushed it out now?

"It could totally destroy it."

"The whatever-it-is? Or the whole house?"

Roddy shrugs.

"What's the loudest, craziest, most spiritual thing you've got?" Eileen asks.

"Honestly, I'd go with Little Richard."

"Play that," she says.

The house convulses while he roots through an album pile. As he slides a record from its jacket, she understands that this is what he has probably wanted all along—to battle toe-to-toe with the house's spirit—instead of the meager payments he'd requested.

Saxophones blare and piano keys clink in flurries. Little Richard starts singing.

Roddy stands still for a few beats before he jumps and does a massive, air-guitar windmill strum. Then, he whips off his car coat and waves it like a matador's cape.

The needle bounces across the record and other voices—*their* voices, Preston and Eileen—rise in volume. She has to hear it all. The worst times of her life. Arguments they had. Arguments they *refused* to have. Shouted fragments overlapping, fighting to rise above Little Richard on a skipping record.

"If you would only..."

"Why do you always..."

"Be reasonable."

A whomp bomp—a whomp bomp—a whomp bomp.

"You're not making sense..."

"Just shut up and listen..."

Jumpback... jumpback... jumpback...

"For God's sake!"

"For the Goddess' sake!"

Bama lama—bama lama—bama lama—bama lama.

"I can't take it!"

"Leave me alone!"

"Why are you always like this?"

Wwwoooooooooooooooooooooooooh

The carpet rips in half, parting like the Red Sea in front of Charlton Heston, rolling into the walls and dragging furniture with it. Nails in the hardwood floor rattle in place, then shoot up—zipping past their heads—into the plaster ceiling. Anything made of glass in the house, from the windows to the dishes to the dial of Eileen's watch, cracks simultaneously. Boards split. Doors fall from hinges.

Eileen scrambles out and across her front yard, leaping into the Ford Falcon's passenger seat. She slides down, pulling her knees to her chest, expecting Roddy to follow her, throw the keys into the ignition, and get them out of there.

Roddy never comes.

She rises to look out the window, putting faith in both the Egyptian pantheon and the 1965 Assembly Line at Ford Motor Company that a single pane of glass will protect her.

Her house splits in half, cracked like the Capitol Dome on the cover of Roddy's Bad Brains record. When the wave of plaster dust rolls by her, it takes a moment to realize she is staring into the exposed interior of her own living room.

There stands Roddy, doing Sixties-type dance steps as the music blasts—flailing his arms and pivoting on the balls of his feet, spinning and pointing, shaking his clasped hands above his head like a champion boxer celebrating victory. Some of the steps she even recognizes, things her father and mother did on those long-ago Saturday nights. The Frug. The Watusi. The Mashed Potato. She knows their names.

Roddy stomps and twists, barely containing a kind of glee the house had never seen while Eileen and Preston inhabited it.

She hears water, a sudden torrential downpour. She expects a deluge of frogs to splatter across the windshield. Instead, a rising carpet of red swells around Roddy's legs.

Blood. They finally got blood. A geyser of it surges from the house's foundation.

For a moment, Roddy seems to float with his chin raised just above the liquid and his fist high in the air. Then, the blood recedes, flowing out into the streets and downspouts, leaving clumps of masonry, broken furniture, and a faint pink tint to the concrete. Roddy stands, crimson head to toe, inside the house's borders, no ceiling above him and only the barest outline of walls surrounding him. He waves at her.

Eileen exits the car, stepping around debris as she crosses the lawn. A deep crater fills the center, with other holes surrounding it. In some spots, mud has vomited out from the basement and over the carpet. Upturned furniture sits half-buried in the ground.

Roddy stands on the only area untouched by the disaster, along the rim of the largest crater, where his records, cords, and gear sit on a sliver of untainted carpet the shape of a crescent moon.

For a moment, he just looks at her without speaking, discerning her mood with what might be genuine empathy, as she surveys the rubble and debris.

"That's never happened before," he tells her.

"Well, there's no way I'm cleaning that up," she says.

All this happened over a decade ago. A year or two earlier, the entirety of Lake Chesterfield in South Saint Louis was devoured by a sinkhole overnight, leaving waterfront McMansions with panoramic views of a six-hundred-acre mud pit. Google it. The stories have cutesy titles like "Woe, Lake Begone" but the disappearance was real as real estate gets.

Maybe that's why the firefighters and insurance guys didn't blink when they tallied the damage with Eileen and Preston the next morning.

The only sign of Roddy was a circle of leaked oil where Horus had been parked. That weekend, he continued his Saturday night show uninterrupted. But the check she left in his office mailbox cleared in a couple of days, and he left one red-ink message on that week's log sheet—*I hope things are better.*

By the time she got his note, Eileen had already quit. She gave the GM two letters—one resigning from her job and another recommending Len for it. She knew Len wouldn't accept if offered, but hoped her good word would give him enough clout to get his request for a new soundboard approved.

Eileen and Preston consulted lawyers within a week of the house's collapse, split the insurance money, and went their separate ways. Preston started staying with Greta before the month was out. It just made sense, he explained. They both needed a roommate.

Here's the real crazy part—had they kept the house and stretched it out a few years, they would have seen their home reduced to half its value, below what they'd paid for it, in a recession that hit even sure-thing areas like Webster Groves. They would have been destitute, underwater, broke.

For anybody else, splitting a house is far more complicated.

Couples implode. They argue over who will get to keep the beloved cat, the sweet Jetta with only nine payments left. A few years pass. The cat dies of leukemia. The Jetta's transmission blows and costs more to fix than to junk it. Even with music, the principle's the same. How many couples ten years ago fought over vast compact disc collections full of box sets, bonus tracks, and hard-to-find rarities that turned valueless in the age of Spotify?

Maybe Eileen and Preston came out ahead.

Eileen doesn't live in St. Louis anymore. If you met her today—*today*, right now—the woman you would see is older, heavier, but carries herself nimbly, with an irrepressible bounce that tosses her graying hair. She's quick to smile at strangers, but not to reveal too much. Her silence doesn't come across as shame but simply a desire to move on. (Only a small trickle of revelations from her over several years made this piece possible.) She doesn't want to tell people where she moved, and rarely discusses the house, her failed marriage, or anything else about that time. Alone but not lonely, adrift but not scared, all she'll say is this—she likes where she lives, in a normal apartment where everything belongs to her. Including all the records.

*See Nathaniel Williams's story "The Record
Collector" online at Metaphorosis.
If you liked it, leave a comment. Authors love
that!
Remember to subscribe to our e-mail updates so
you'll know when new stories are posted.*

About the story

I went to college with a ton of Saint Louis folks and
over the years heard many vignettes about the area.
The stuff in my story about the Exorcist hospital and
the Lake Chesterfield sinkhole is all true. Saint Louis is
also the home of Beatle Bob, the nationally known
music superfan who attends concerts almost nightly,
always decked in vintage 60s gear. (If you played in an
area band and Bob attended your show, it meant
something.) There's a little Beatle Bob in Roddy, even
though the character ultimately asserted a more
unique persona as I wrote him. And, as a displaced
Midwesterner, I miss the area. I've spent time recently
thinking of all those Gen-Xers who lived around there
in the early 2000s (many good friends and mentors)
and the ups and downs they've seen since I moved
away. That's in there too.

A question for the author

Q: Do you have a garden? Have you ever grown your own food?

A: No. I'm ill-suited to nurture plants. I can barely keep children and pets alive, and they at least tell you when they're hungry.

About the author

Nathaniel Williams was born in Kansas City and currently teaches technical writing and journalism at the University of California, Davis. He's worked as a radio announcer, grant writer, and musician, and has spent the past decade or so researching rare American science fiction in dime novels from the nineteenth century. He is a graduate of the Writers Workshop at the Gunn Center for the Study of Science Fiction.

www.nathanielwms.com, @nathanielwms

Zsezzyn, Who Is Not a God

Jennifer Shelby

A lone man watches over the universe, and the pen he wields contains the power to erase from existence all he deems unworthy. His daughter, Zsezzyn, plays at his feet.

She likes to watch him work — the steadily deepening crease on his brow, the scales on which he measures a balance of right, wrong, and the gray that lives between. One day, he will bequeath his pen to her, and this cave where the universe is mapped out above their heads will become her sacred place as it is his. "This is the way of gods," he tells her.

For now, Zsezzyn frolics beneath the silver pinpricks of the stars, nervous of the darkness that broods between them. At night she dreams the darkness overwhelms her and she runs to the stars for comfort. She spends her childhood shooting arrows with Orion, pouring cups of shadow from twin Dippers, learning her first letter from the W of Cassiopeia.

The stars are her universe, until they disappear. One at a time, the darkness devours them. Zsezzyn traces her fingers along the space where a star once twinkled, struggling to understand, afraid to ask her father why tears run down his cheeks. "Where did the star go, Papa?"

He gathers her into his arms and takes her outside the cave to show her the night sky. The stars are bigger here, but so is the darkness. Zsezzyn shrinks into his embrace. "The people who lived by the lost star committed terrible deeds," he tells her. "The burden of protecting the universe from such people falls to us and we must not take this responsibility lightly. My grandfather found the threat of punishment alone kept peace. My father had to wield our family's power twice in his lifetime and I am already past that. Though we strive to use this power sparingly, it has made us many enemies." He turns his face away from her and stares into the darkness. "There are those who would take our power for their own and use it against us." He pats her hand. "But I will keep you safe from them."

Zsezzyn does not ask for details.

Years pass, until one day Zsezzyn notices Orion's Belt has disappeared. She turns to her father, to ask what happened, but anger simmers in the dimming starlight surrounding him and she keeps her questions to herself. This is the last day she spends playing in the cave.

When she is old enough, her father tells her everything. "Your great-grandfather made the ink for our pen from a pool of dark matter he discovered at the bottom of a black hole. You need only take up this pen and ink over a star to remove it from the universe."

Zsezzyn is stricken to see how many stars are gone, how dark the cave has grown. Her father follows her gaze and sighs. "My grandfather built this cave to end the chaos of the universe. When he died, the burden of power fell to my father, then to me, as one day it will fall to you." His voice grows firm. "Yet more and more there are those who wish to strip us of our godship. This, I do not allow."

Zsezzyn does not try to hide her horror. "But Papa, there are so few stars left. You told me we must wield our power sparingly."

His face hardens, he clutches his pen to his chest. "One day you will understand."

"Will there be any stars left then?" Zsezzyn asks.

"The only star we need to survive is our own sun."

Zsezzyn looks at the pen in his hand, worn and old, a fountain pen carved from the core of a comet, its nib stained dark, a small window in the barrel warning it is low on ink. But that doesn't matter when so little stars remain.

"We are gods," he tells her. "They are twinkles in a cave."

She turns to go and does not look back as she leaves her father, and then her world, behind. Far from the shelter of the cave, from an asteroid she forges a pen of her own.

One by one, the last stars disappear, until only her sun remains. The darkness of the universe around the asteroid brings back her childhood fears. The void pulsates with something she cannot see, licking at her fright, threatening to swallow more than stars. Zsezzyn stares into the empty black, daring it to consume her, and nothing happens.

When at last her pen is done, she travels to the sun that gave life to her world, the lone star her father has not found fault with. She steps upon the surface of the star. Its fires dare not burn her, for the flames know whose daughter she is and what he has done to a thousand other stars. The star guides her safely to its molten core, where its light should blind, its heat should melt, its heart should devour her. Instead Zsezzyn's fears are burned away, replaced by a scorching, fiery will. She takes out the cartridge she has made for her pen and hesitates. Lifting her head and gazing into the star fire, she asks, "May I?"

The star consents with a small nudge of flame. Zsezzyn plunges the cartridge into the star's liquid heart. When she is done, she stands, pocketing the instrument with a surge of hope.

She meets her father in his cave, her pen bright in the darkness. "I made this for us, Papa, to restore what we have lost." Zsezzyn holds her breath, clinging to the memory of the tears he once shed in this cave.

He considers her pen, his expression shifting from furious to uncertain. He draws out his own pen and holds it in his palms, trembling as he looks from the tool to the darkness of the cave. Where once Zsezzyn sensed his anger simmer in the starlight she now feels his regret unspool into the darkness. "My work is done," he tells her. "Our family's legacy falls to you now."

"Papa?" Zsezzyn reaches for him, but she is too late. He grips his pen in his fists and snaps it in half. What remains of the ink darkens his fingers briefly before he disappears like all his stars.

The broken pieces of his pen clatter to the floor. Zsezzyn stares at them a long time. Her great-grandfather once believed this pen held the power to protect the universe, and it did, for a time. Its corruption did not begin until much later and with it came a darkness which consumed her father whole.

When Zsezzyn's grief subsides, she studies the cave walls, sifting through the constellations of her memory. Orion's belt twinkled there, one, two, three. With a trembling hand, she presses the pen's nib against the wall and draws a star. Silver light pierces the darkness. Another, and another. All of Orion, Cassiopeia, and over there a Dipper, the big one.

Zsezzyn falls into a frenzy of creation, filling the universe with the stars it lost. A myriad forgotten lives resume. A billion worlds fall back into the orbit of their reborn suns. She adds new stars for the sheer, majestic wonder of it. Hours pass before she steps back to admire the universe, the cave bright with silver light.

Her father might not have been proud, but Zsezzyn is no god, she is only someone who wields a powerful tool. She places the pen on the floor of the cave and steps outside. The universe stretches overhead, bright again with stars and life, and bold with the light of the incoming comet she drew to seal up the cave forever.

See Jennifer Shelby's story "Zsezzyn, Who Is Not a God" online at Metaphorosis.
If you liked it, leave a comment. Authors love that!
Remember to subscribe to our e-mail updates so you'll know when new stories are posted.

About the story

My toddler has a toy turtle which lights up and projects stars onto the ceiling. Like most kids her age, she's nervous of the dark and often turns it on when I'm putting her to bed. One night I blocked out several of the stars with my hand and she started to cry. As I tried to imagine how she might have perceived those missing stars, I found the story.

Zsezzyn's story is also about a damaged inheritance. I listen to what scientists say about climate change and wonder how my children will react to the world they inherit. Zsezzyn's father believes he's handing her a legacy to be proud of, but to Zsezzyn it is the ruins of a universe, devoid of potential.

A question for the author

Q: Do you live near where you were born? Have you traveled much?

A: I was born in Nova Scotia, a province in Eastern Canada, and currently live in New Brunswick. Looking out my window I can see Nova Scotia across the Bay of Fundy. New Brunswick is where I grew up and the smell of the Bay, dramatic shoreline, and deep forests are home. I moved to Central and Western Canada for my education but always gravitated back to New Brunswick again.

As a child I travelled through most of the United States in the back of my parents' Volkswagen. I gawked at New York City and the Grand Canyon in between Battleship games with my brother and a handful of Nancy Drew novels.

In my early twenties I spent three months in rural Costa Rica as part of a conservation volunteer group. I treasure the experiences I had in the rainforests there and the beautiful communities that welcomed us into their lives. There were blankets of fireflies along the edges of one forest that will forever haunt my dreams.

About the author

Jennifer Shelby hunts for stories in the beetle undergrowth of fairy-infested forests. She fishes for them in the dark space between the stars. Zsezzyn, Who is Not a God's publication in *Metaphorosis* is part of her ongoing catch-and-release program. You can learn more at jennifershelby.blog or on Twitter @jenniferdshelby

The Woman Who Brought Love to Death

Kathryn Yelinek

Gudrun plunked herself down in the grass, her back against the side of the sod house. The guests were feasting, and the funeral ale was flowing, so she could indulge her grief a moment. Almighty gods, had Ketill been dead a week already?

In the distance, the last of the smoke from his funeral pyre drifted over the horse fields. Beyond that, clear on the horizon, lay the green hill of Graenheth. Souls went into that hill on their way to the Forever Shore. Right now, Ketill would be inside, beyond the setting sun, past the troll who guarded the entrance to the land of the dead. He would be roaming the endless expanse of beach, sea cliffs, and tide pools, one soul among millions. A soul could wander that beach forever, searching in vain for a beloved.

She knew without a doubt that he was there, beyond her reach, because she could see the love-lines they shared. Theirs were still thick as whale bones and brilliant scarlet, a testament to their passion. They ran from her out across the hills and waving grass, translucent red ribbons that ran unerringly toward Graenheth. So Ketill truly was there, even though her mind refused to grasp it. She thought she might go mad with the need to touch him again.

Around her, as the guests roared and lifted overflowing tankards to the midnight sun, the love-lines of friends and family filled the valley. The ones for Ketill all stretched west, toward Graenheth and the Forever Shore. Yellow for familial love, green for friendship, their width and depth of color showed how close each person had been to Ketill. They stretched through the air like bits of a splintered rainbow, he'd been so beloved.

How she wanted to follow the lines, to track Ketill down and throw her arms around him. They'd been a good pair, the two of them, since he brought her from Egleby five years before. And she would follow them if she could. Here in the valley the islanders thought her a witch because she could see the love-lines and they could not. Her life would be hard among them now, without Ketill's protection. But she couldn't go into the hill, not now. She would not dishonor Ketill by cutting short his full year of mourning rites.

As if to reinforce how alone she was, Solvi, Ketill's son from his first marriage, banged his tankard on the funeral bench and cried, "We'll avenge my father! We'll see justice done!"

The guests roared, and hard glances turned toward her. As usual. She should stay silent, but her eyes ached from weeping, and she was in no mood for Solvi's self-centered boasting.

"How will you avenge him?" she asked, low. "Desecrate the horse that struck him?"

Silence, and for a moment she thought the guests were pondering how best to dismember Tanni, Ketill's favorite horse. They'd already slaughtered the poor beast for what he'd done.

Then: "That horse never hurt him before!"

"No horse ever hurt him."

"He was the island's best horse breaker."

"Horse musta been magicked!"

Solvi raised his hand, still clutching his eating knife, and pointed a shaking finger at her. "You were the last person in the horse fields before the stallion kicked him. What do you have to say for yourself, witch?"

She opened her mouth, snapped it shut. At the time of Ketill's death, she'd been following a pair of love-lines, intent on discovering who shared a secret crush. In Egleby, her matchmaking stall had thrived, and she missed the work. But these guests with their spears and axes didn't want to hear about love-lines.

"I did not kill him."

"What were you doing in the field?"

The looks they gave her—anger, fear, hatred—she knew what they meant. Ketill was burned, his soul safely beyond the setting sun on the Forever Shore. No matter what they did to her, his ghost would not haunt them.

She shot to her feet. Just in time, as she scrambled to dodge a rock that thumped into the turf wall where her head had been.

She ran. A stone bashed her shoulder, sending her tumbling into the grass. A cheer went up, and she scrambled to her feet, terror drying her tears. She sprinted past the horse fields, past Ketill's cooling pyre, the jeers loud behind her. Her shoulder stung.

She crested the hill and plunged into the valley below, plowing through waving grass. Finally, two valleys over, she stopped. Panting, her hand to the cramp in her side, she scanned the horizon from the glacier-capped volcanos behind to the far-distant sea in front. No one was following; she was alone with the love-lines.

Instinctively she stepped toward Graenheth, toward Ketill. She had no reason not to go there now. By chasing her away, Solvi had exiled her. No farmstead would give her shelter, no ship captain would grant her passage. Without supplies, she would not survive the winter or complete the mourning rites. Better to drown herself and forego the misery.

But dead, she wouldn't see love-lines. The priests were clear: no unnatural abilities survived death. And she had to see the lines. Without them she would never find Ketill, not on the endless shore.

If she wanted to see him again, to touch him, she'd have to go now, lack of supplies be damned.

"Ketill," she whispered, "I'm coming."

She struck out across the rippling grasses, Graenheth small and sheer in the distance, a good day's journey away. Hour after hour, she walked, beyond sleep, driven by longing, until Graenheth loomed tall, a flat-topped hill of green and gold jutting from the ground. Two ravens called from its top, a grim sign. She shaded her eyes, though her arms felt heavy as boulders. Her mind was muddy, refusing to focus. But she'd made it, even if she had no idea how to get inside the hill.

She eyed Ketill's love-lines, hoping they would show her. Except they didn't go inside. They kept going, past Graenheth to the shore behind.

She gaped. Was Ketill's soul lost?

No, all the love-lines led past the hill to the shore. Old, faded lines and new, sharp ones alike.

So, if he wasn't where all the priests and his family said he was, where was he?

She trudged around the base of the hill and down the grassy slope behind until she stood on the edge of a sea cliff, waves crashing below. To her left, a river drained into the sea, ice chunks from the distant glacier riding high. In the bay, black rock arches braced the shore and stood as sea stacks in the water. The love-lines flowed past them, converging on one black pinnacle of rock halfway to the horizon.

"I don't know how to get there, either," a voice said.

Gudrun jumped. Crouched in a rock cleft was a small black-and-white dog. Green friendship love-lines ran from it to the black pinnacle and back.

"You're trying to cross over too, yes?" the dog asked when she didn't respond.

Gudrun breathed hard through her nose. Too many shocks, one after another, were making her slow.

She picked her words carefully. "I'm sorry for your loss."

The dog cocked its head. "You can smell the passing souls, too?"

"I see the love you shared with someone now in the rock."

"My horse friend, Astrid. She had saddle sores and didn't want to be ridden, so the man hit her until she didn't get up. I miss her."

"I'm sorry," Gudrun said again, now for all humans, because they did terrible things to animals. "How is it I understand you?"

"In choosing to come here, we've taken the first step into Death's domain. Things are different here. Why do humans ask such obvious questions?"

"It's not obvious to me. Humans and dogs experience the world in different ways."

The dog nodded, satisfied. "My name's Bjorn. Whom are you trying to reach?"

"My husband, Ketill. My name is Gudrun."

Bjorn barked, grinning a doggie grin. "That's why you smell so good!" He limped toward her and pressed his nose into her leg. His head came about to her knee. "The man had a daughter named Gudrun. She was kind to me, until she clasped hands with another and moved away."

"Did 'the man' do this to you?" Gudrun reached for his front right paw. It oozed from a puncture wound.

Bjorn snapped at her, growling. She jerked her hand back and pressed it to her chest.

At once, his ears and tail went down. He slunk toward her, eyes wide as a puppy's. "I'm sorry. It hurts."

"It looks deep." She sat on her heels. "May I see?"

Slowly he held out his paw. She took it carefully, but he whimpered.

"It'll be my death," he said. "I smell it."

He spoke truth. The wound was far along and festering. She pulled the kerchief from her hair and wrapped it around his paw.

"So you don't hurt it more."

He licked her chin, and her face warmed in delight. It was the first happiness she'd felt in a week. Just like that, tendrils of green friendship stretched between them.

"It's good to have a nice human to travel with," Bjorn said, sitting back on his haunches. "How do you think we can get over?"

She frowned at the waves crashing below. "It's too far to swim, even if we could get past those breakers."

"Do you have a boat?"

"No, and no one would lend me one." She hesitated. "You—you could just end your life, you know."

He blinked at her. "Maybe for humans. We dogs don't do that. Why haven't you?"

"I won't see love-lines if I'm dead. And the love-lines will lead me straight to Ketill. No wandering the Shore."

"Oh! I'm staying with you. So how do we get over?"

"I don't know." She couldn't bear that this might be the end, that she would have to face Solvi's wrath instead of reconciling with Ketill. "If only we could walk on the love-lines. They would take us right over."

Bjorn's ears perked up. "That's perfect. Let's walk now."

"We can't. The lines are light, like a rainbow. We can't walk on light."

"Oh." His ears dropped. "I hoped they were more solid."

"No." She tapped her chin, thinking. They couldn't swim. They didn't have a boat, and she wasn't about to go back. But she did have a talking dog, so maybe she should start thinking of other ways around her problem. "Since you can talk to me, could you talk some seals or whales into taking us out to the rock?"

He cocked his head. "Maybe, if they were here, and if we had something they wanted."

Neither was true, so she tried another direction. "You said we were in Death's domain. How did you know this?"

He whimpered and ducked his head. "The man—he was a sorcerer."

Gudrun shivered. Sorcerers were dark and dangerous men who used runes to write evil spells. No wonder Bjorn had whimpered.

And yet...

She knelt down. "Is there anything else the man told you that could help us? A spell to calm the waters? Or to conjure a boat?"

Bjorn growled deep in his throat. "He knew a spell to magnify fear."

Her heart went out to him. "I'm sorry. I didn't mean to bring back bad memories. I won't ask again."

Bjorn nodded, tight, then nuzzled her knee so she knew they were all right. She stood, surveying the distant rock, and mulled over his words.

As a matchmaker, she'd learned enough writing to carve a rune for the occasional love charm. And now she knew there was a spell that could increase fear. So maybe here in Death's domain, where things were different, there was a way to use her rune to help them. She wasn't sure how, but it was a start.

"Think you could get me a fist-sized rock? As flat as possible?" She pointed to the riverbank.

Bjorn thumped his tail. "I love fetching!"

He hobbled to the river, limping so badly that Gudrun regretted asking him. Then he gave a yip of delight and grabbed a rock with his jaws.

He dropped it at her feet. "I got it! Didn't I do well?"

She laughed at his glee. "Very well."

As she picked up the rock, she realized she'd just laughed for the first time in a week. It felt good.

"So what are you going to do?" Bjorn asked.

"I know one rune to use in love charms. I use it to strengthen love-lines. I wonder if that can help us."

Bjorn nodded. "The man said words when he carved his runes. I didn't like to listen. They hurt my ears."

"Words have power. It's true." Witch. Dead. Justice. These weren't spells, but they had changed her life.

Her eating knife hung from a brooch on her dress. Thank the gods she had adopted the islander custom of carrying it with her at all times. She untied the string that held it and used it to carve into the stone the rune she knew, whispering the spell to strengthen love-lines. When she was done, she surveyed the love-lines in front of her. She couldn't choose her line or Bjorn's, because those would move with them as they crossed over the sea. She needed a line that would stay still. She needed—there. A scarlet line as wide as a narrow branch ran east into the volcanos. It came from someone on the other side of the peaks, so it should not move much.

She prayed and jabbed the rock into the red line. The line flared, growing brighter and wider, but the rock fell through. It thudded on the ground.

Her heart sank. Bjorn whined and nosed the rock.

She picked it up. "Maybe a spell to thicken a woman's womb, something that will make the line more solid."

Again she whispered her words and jabbed the rock in. This time it sank slowly through the line before thudding to the ground.

"It almost worked!" Bjorn said. "Try again."

She did, this time with a spell to stiffen a man during love-play. But again the rock sank through before landing by her feet.

Bjorn hung his head. He didn't bother to push the rock toward her this time. "What else can we do?"

"I don't know," she whispered. She picked up the rock and squeezed it tightly. "I don't know any other spells to try."

She wished she could ask what spells the sorcerer had used, but she had promised not to. She didn't dare suggest they ask the sorcerer for help. Together, she and Bjorn would have to come up with another plan.

Oh.

Together. Yes! She had overlooked a crucial aspect of the love-lines. They were connected at both ends, flavored by both the lover and beloved. On this island, that usually meant male and female. But she had tried a spell for each gender in turn. Maybe if she combined them, it would work.

"Almighty gods," she prayed. "Make this work."

She breathed deep, intoned a combination of the spells, then jabbed the rock into the line. It held.

She had a moment to marvel, then Bjorn nosed her leg.

"It worked! Let's go!"

"Patience." She ran her hand along the solid ribbon of red, testing it, hardly believing her words had worked. "It's only as wide as a branch, and slippery as ice." Which made a sort of sense, since rainbows happened when sunlight hit spray, and water turned into ice. So when she'd stiffened the line, it had followed its rainbow nature and crystalized into a ribbon of ice. She would rather the line had turned into something less slippery, but she'd take what she could get.

Buoyed, she retied her knife and tucked it on its string into her neckline so it would not get in her way as they crossed. Then she hiked up her skirts and climbed onto the red ribbon, straddling it. It was cold and slick against her fingers, and she wished she had her ice spikes.

When the ice didn't break under her weight, she boosted Bjorn up behind her. "Hold onto my skirts. I don't want you falling."

Bjorn whined, but he snagged the hem of her skirt as she scooched forward her first hesitant armlengths. The ribbon was slick and narrow, but there was no other way. Bjorn's claws clicked behind her, and she thought about this rather than peering into the blue-gray waters below, rather than dwelling on how cold her hands and legs were. If only she had her mittens.

The black pinnacle of rock grew closer, but the journey seemed never ending. No matter how she shifted along, the ribbon seemed to stretched ever longer. The sun inched across the sky, past the midday mark, and still she was creeping along over the blue-gray water far below, and now her skirts and fingers were wet.

She gasped. "The ice is melting!"

She crept faster, her palms slapping the ribbon. If only it were wider. If only she could run.

A crack sounded, a breaking of the air, and the ribbon swayed. She grabbed hold, her heartbeat thrumming in all the corners of her body.

"It's crumbling in the middle!" Bjorn yelled.

She moved as fast as she could, Bjorn yipping that the ice was cracking behind his tail, until black showed beneath red, and she collapsed on a ledge of black rock. Bjorn nosed into her side, whimpering. She held him, savoring his warmth. The love-line cracked and popped and then it was nothing but a translucent ribbon again. Raising her hand, she passed her fingers through it.

The ledge could fit her and Bjorn and not much more. Warmth radiated up, returning the heat of the sun, but the air was chilly and the wind biting. Bits of gray lichen spotted the rock, and the air smelled of bird droppings, but no birds perched nearby. On this small space, it was just her and Bjorn and a startlingly long drop off the edge to the foaming waves below.

After a moment to warm her fingers in Bjorn's fur, she ran her hands over the rock face at the back of the ledge. The love-line went into the rock at chest height. Other lines—red and yellow and green—dove in around it.

"How do we get in?" Bjorn hobbled up beside her.

The rock was warm from the sun and smooth from the wind, but hard and —"Oh! A door!"

Hidden in a split in the rock, a black corridor barely as wide as her shoulders led into darkness. Far at the end, light gleamed, colored red and yellow and green by love-lines.

"Think that's the Forever Shore?" Bjorn asked, tilting his head toward the light.

"I wish, but I think we have a ways to go. Past the setting sun and a guardian troll, right?"

Bjorn sighed and nodded.

"Let me carry you," Gudrun said. The kerchief around his paw was nearly soaked through.

"I can walk," Bjorn protested, but not too much, and he snuggled against her shoulder as she stepped into the corridor.

It wasn't far. After a walk through cool, musty rock, the corridor took a sharp elbow turn to the right. She peeked around the rock and met painfully bright light.

"Ow!" She jerked back, slamming her eyes shut.

Bjorn nuzzled her shoulder. "Are you okay?"

Back in the corridor, she blinked, spots dancing in her vision. "I'm all right, but I don't know how to walk through that. If I look too long, I'll go blind."

"Can you feel your way?"

"Maybe, but if I fall, we're both going down. And I don't want either of us getting burned or blinded or worse. That's the setting sun we have to get past, isn't it?"

Bjorn whined, his ears back, but he said, "Let me lead. I'll sniff out the path, and only have to peek a little."

"But your paw..."

"Better my paw than your sight. We need that. Here, tie some cloth as a rope around my middle so I can lead you."

There had to be a better way, but she couldn't think of one. She pulled her trusty knife from her neckline, chopped cloth from her skirt, and tied the leash around his chest. She tied another bandage around his paw, too. "Lead on."

It was disconcerting, walking with her eyes closed, the tugging of the leash telling her to go right or left. The air grew warm, then uncomfortably hot. She wiped her face and wished for water. How big could the sun be? Shouldn't they be past it by now? Still she padded over rock as fine as salt, bracing herself for the lurch of the leash that would signal disaster.

Then the air cooled, the brightness dimmed, and Bjorn yipped that she could open her eyes.

He led her out a doorway to a narrow path. Sunshine streamed down, not too bright. On either side were black rock shapes—columns, mounds, keyholes through which she could see the summer-blue sky. The white full moon rode high beside the sun.

Seeing that, she shivered. "We're not in the old world anymore."

Bjorn wriggled. "I hear waves. Just beyond that bend. The Forever Shore must be close!"

She untied his leash, and he surged ahead, then froze, his hair standing on edge.

"What?" Gudrun demanded.

She was answered by a troll rounding the bend.

He stood twice her height and three times her breadth, with black knobby skin to match the rocks. "Go away. You're not dead."

He was much larger than she'd expected. Still she said, "Let us pass. We made the journey. It's your duty to let us pass."

"My duty is to keep the land of the dead for the dead. Now go." He shooed with his hands.

Bjorn growled, light glinting on his teeth. He jumped, biting into the troll's shin. The troll hissed and swatted, barely missing as Bjorn ducked away.

"Stop!" Gudrun called. Bjorn was staggering, and he might have been a gnat for all his bite had done. The path showed red where he walked.

Bjorn glared at her, but he must have thought better of his attack, because his ears went down, and he limped to her side. The troll strode forward, forcing them back up the path. Black rock rose sharp and straight on both sides. The door to the corridor loomed at their backs.

"I'll give you one of my brooches," she told the troll, "if you let us pass. See how it sparkles?"

"What good would that do? The rocks sparkle even more."

"What about this glass bead necklace? My husband gave it to me as a wedding present."

The troll snorted, making Bjorn start. "I don't need your wedding present. Go away."

"You could have my knife," she said, though it pained her. "It's small and sharp."

"Take your knife and leave me alone!"

At the forcefulness of his cry, she backed into the brightly lit corridor, Bjorn stumbling behind her. But as she looked despairingly out to the path they'd left behind, a red love-line caught her attention. It ran from the troll to a column of rock.

The troll was in love with a rock? No—a more brilliant line ran from him to the Forever Shore. His beloved was there.

"Come on," Bjorn whispered, pressing against her. "Maybe we can get in another way."

What other way was there?

"Whom do you love?" she asked the troll, hoping to buy time. "Who's waiting for you on the Shore?"

The troll froze. He stared at her, his black nostrils flared.

"You love someone very much," she continued, stepping back onto the path, puzzling out the connection between his two love lines, one a pale echo of the other. "And someone—no some*thing* she gave you, something you connect with her, is over in the rock."

The troll narrowed his eyes. "What do you know of my loves?"

"I see the love-lines between people and the things they love. A line connects you to something over there. Is it a jewel? A letter?" She guessed wildly, not knowing what trolls held dear. Then a thought occurred: "A knife? Did you lose your knife? You don't carry one." This even though he had a knife loop on his belt like the islander men had. "Is that why you yelled at me when I offered mine?"

The troll's eyes grew as wide as the moon. "If you get my knife back, I'll let you stay. Both of you."

She clasped her hands together, full of hope. "Where is it?"

The troll pointed to the top of one of the rocky mounds, nearly as tall as he was. "It fell into a crack in the rock, and I can't get it out."

"I'll try," Gudrun said. "Only I don't know how to get up there."

The troll picked her up. She gasped, but then she was on top of the mound. The crack in the rock was thin, but not so thin she couldn't reach her arm inside. At the bottom, the knife lay on a bed of snow that hadn't melted, even in endless daylight. It was big—maybe three times bigger than hers—and thin and black as the rock.

She lay down and stretched her arm inside, but she couldn't reach. So she sat up, untied her knife and angled it into the crack. Maybe she could use it to tip the troll's knife up. But even with her knife, her reach was too short.

Desperate, she snipped the string that had held her knife. Tying the end into a loop, she lowered the lasso into the crack. If she could snag the knife, she could lift it up. If—ha! The loop caught.

She pulled, careful, careful, the black blade sparkling in the faint light. The string tightened, and snap! The knife fell back on its bed of snow.

"No!" She hauled the string up. It had been cut cleanly in half. How sharp the blade was!

Something touched her leg. She flinched, nearly dropping her string.

"I can get it!" Bjorn said.

"How'd you get up here?"

"Hallr." He nodded to the troll, who was plucking impatiently at his tunic.

"The blade's really sharp. And your paw's hurt. Are you sure you can get it?"

"I got us past the sun. I'll get the knife."

"Be careful."

Bjorn nodded and squeezed down into the crack. It was very narrow, but he was a small dog. As Gudrun held her breath, he jumped down, leaving red footprints on the lip of the rock. Then he yipped once, twice.

"Bjorn, are you okay?"

No answer. Had he yipped in victory? Pain?

Then he was wriggling up, scrabbling with his back legs. She grabbed hold and hauled him up.

"Did you get it?"

He whimpered. The knife clattered onto the rock.

"You got it!"

Blood splattered her arm. So much blood. Where was it coming from?

She turned Bjorn in her arms. "How are you hurt? Is it your paw?"

He whined. Blood matted his snout. "Find Astrid," he whispered.

She struggled to understand him. Holding him close, she saw the deep cuts that crisscrossed his lips.

"You were supposed to grab the handle!"

"Couldn't reach," he slurred. His head flopped against her wrist. His eyes fluttered.

"Bjorn!" She pressed the edge of her skirt against his lips. Blood soaked the cloth. His tail flicked limply. "Hold on, Bjorn."

"You got it!" The troll, Hallr, plucked up his knife. "Is the dog okay?"

"His name's Bjorn," she snapped. He wasn't moving. She laid her hand on his chest. It didn't move, either. She bowed her head.

"I'm sorry," Hallr said.

"He was a good dog," she whispered, fighting back tears. "He only wanted to be with his friend."

"Now he can, if he can find her."

As Hallr spoke, Bjorn stood up. Not the Bjorn that lay on the rocks. Out of that Bjorn, a new Bjorn rose. He was still small and furry and black and white. Anywhere else he would have been invisible to her, but here, so close to the Forever Shore, he was only faintly translucent, like linen in the sun.

He stepped one paw and then another out of his body. When he stood free, he shook himself. Love-lines ran from him to her and to the Forever Shore.

"My paw doesn't hurt!" Wriggling with excitement, he pushed his nose into her arm.

It felt like any dog nose, only dry. Hesitantly she wrapped her arms around him, feeling the coarse curls of his fur. He felt like any other dog, except he had no smell she could smell, and that made her sad.

"You weren't supposed to die," she said into his fur. "Not now."

"But I got the knife." He licked her cheek. "Let's find Astrid and your husband." Pulling away, he stepped to the edge of the rock column. With a doggie grin, he walked over the edge.

She shrieked, but he landed lightly on the path below.

"Let's go!"

Too many shocks, she thought. She looked back at the body of the Bjorn she had known. Like all bodies, it looked smaller, as if the part of Bjorn that paced the path had been excised. She picked up a few pebbles, piled them by his head—for remembrance, for a life lived too short—then stepped onto Hallr's proffered palm. He set her on the trail.

They followed the path. Waves crashed in the distance. She prayed to any god who would listen that both Astrid and Ketill were close, that Bjorn's sacrifice would bear fruit.

They rounded the bend in the path, and the Shore opened before them: black sand as far as she could see, waves lapping the beach, black rock columns jutting from the water beyond. Souls dotted the beach by themselves or in groups of two, some sitting on the sand, others walking by the water. Love-lines turned the air into a patchwork of rainbows.

"So, um, about you being here." Hallr did not meet her eye. "I—"

"Hallr, what is that living woman doing here?"

The voice split the air like river ice cracking. A person strode up the beach, cloak flapping, shoulder-length hair blowing in a wind Gudrun couldn't feel. Souls trailed behind like ducklings following their mother.

"Please," one soul said, tugging the person's cloak, "tell me where my son is."

"And my fiancée!" another soul said. "Where is she?"

"Sweetie, look," Hallr said as the person approached. Ignoring the clustering souls, he held out his knife. "These two got my knife back."

"You shouldn't have lost it in the first place, darling." The person spoke harshly, but Hallr only beamed at the knife. "And it doesn't explain why she is here."

"I, ah, told them I'd let them stay if they did."

"The dog can stay, not her."

"Please," Gudrun said, her voice cracking. She had never expected to speak to Death. "I need to be with my husband. The community thinks I caused his death. I'm exiled. I have nowhere else to go."

"You may look for him when you are dead." Death swept out a skeletal hand to indicate the clustering souls. "Otherwise, you go."

"I need to be with him now."

"Then you die."

"If I'm dead, I won't be able to find him."

Death tsked. "My shores are vast. Being dead or alive makes no difference in your ability to find someone. Even I don't know where everyone is." This was reinforced with a glower at the souls.

"But I can find him easily. I see the love we share. I can follow our love-lines straight to him."

A few souls gasped. Death arced a thick brow. "Do not fib to me."

"If I prove it, will you let me stay?"

"Only if you are dead."

Gudrun clenched her fists. There had to be another way. "How is he here?" She pointed to Hallr, who was still beaming at his knife. "He's not dead."

"He works for me."

"I could work for you. I could reunite souls with those they love."

Death harrumphed, but the loitering souls exclaimed happily, and Hallr set a hand on Death's arm. "Let her try. You're always complaining you can't get anything done with all these souls pestering you."

"All right." Death folded thin arms in a dare. "Show me."

Yes! Gudrun spun to the left, where both her and Bjorn's love-lines led. "Come on, Bjorn. Astrid's this way, too."

Bjorn barked, his ears up, and bounded down the beach.

If only she could run that fast, race down the sand to Ketill. Instead she set a brisk pace, walking as quickly as she dared. Hallr followed, yammering on about the people they passed, while Death walked silent at his side, the lonely souls trailing behind. Wave after wave crashed on their right, and Gudrun was remembering how tired she was when one of the love-lines veered off to the left, up a small hill with evergreens bordering the shore.

"Bjorn! Astrid's up there."

Barking madly, Bjorn tore up the hill. A moment later, a horse whinnied from the trees. The two met nose to nose at the crest of the hill, Bjorn bestowing slobbering kisses on his friend.

Gudrun pressed her hands to her chest, overjoyed. Then she saw her own love-line angling off the beach up ahead. She ran.

She rounded the next curve of the beach, and there he was, sitting on an outcropping of rock, watching the herd of horses to which Astrid now belonged, green friendship lines running from him to the herd.

Her mouth was dry. Her throat squeezed tight. She called, "Ketill!"

He tensed. He turned around. His body went still in shock, then he was sprinting down the hill to her.

"Gudrun, what are you doing here?"

She wrapped her arms around him. This was his hug, the scratch of his beard on her neck, the curve of his back under her hands. He no longer smelled like himself, either. She missed that, but still it was him.

"I followed the love-lines."

"And I'm glad you did, but why are you here? You're not dead." He pulled back to frown down at her in concern.

As usual, she couldn't hide her worries from him. "Everyone thinks I magicked your horse, that I murdered you. They exiled me."

His face darkened. "The idiots. Of course you didn't murder me. It was an accident. I just wish I knew why Tanni kicked me."

That she could help with. This she had been born to do. A shiver of excitement coursed through her as she beckoned Ketill up the hill he'd just come down, following the vivid green friendship lines she recognized. At the top she shaded her eyes, tracing the line into the distance, to where a brown horse stood by itself, half hidden by trees, away from the rest of the herd. As if it were ashamed. Or in mourning.

She put two fingers in her mouth and whistled just as Ketill had shown her.

The horse's head came up. Well trained, it trotted up the hill.

"Tanni?" Ketill whispered, aghast, as the stallion approached, head low.

"They killed him," she said, "for what he did. I'm sorry."

Ketill's face was haggard. He held out his palm. Tanni shied away, then his ears came up and he lipped Ketill's palm.

"I'm sorry," Tanni murmured. Ketill had been on the Shore long enough he didn't flinch at a talking horse. "I felt a small earthquake—"

"I didn't feel one," Ketill protested.

"You humans often don't." Tanni switched his tail. "This one scared me. I didn't mean to hit you."

"It's okay," Ketill said, wrapping his arms around Tanni's neck. He offered Gudrun his hand across Tanni's withers. "I'm sorry for what they've put you through."

She took his hand. "Me, too."

Death had climbed the hill behind them, followed by Hallr and the souls. Love-lines swarmed the air around them, an enticing array.

"Impressive," Death said, grudgingly.

"Thank you." She squeezed Ketill's hand and faced Death. "So I may stay?"

"If you truly wish it."

"Please!" one soul said, scrambling out from behind Death. "Find my son!"

"No, my betrothed!" another called.

"Better hurry," Hallr said. "More souls are coming down the corridor. They'll have folks for you to find, too."

She took a deep breath. Only now did she realize how big a job she was taking on—the souls newly arriving would leave little time to reunite the souls already clamoring around Death. She could work every moment of every day and still have an endless supply of souls to match. And when would she find time for Ketill?

"We'll come with you," he said, rubbing Tanni's nose. "Won't we?" Tanni whinnied.

She let out her breath. It would be a big job, but it was good work, which needed to be done.

"Okay," she said to the soul closest to Death. "Whom are you looking for?"

See Kathryn Yelinek's story "The Woman Who Brought Love to Death" online at Metaphorosis. If you liked it, leave a comment. Authors love that!
Remember to subscribe to our e-mail updates so you'll know when new stories are posted.

About the story

I've had the image of a woman who could see love in my head for years, but I couldn't find the right story for the character. I tried everything—romance, murder mystery, you name it. But none of the stories worked. A few were downright embarrassing, now that I look back on them. Still, I kept coming back to the idea of what would it be like to see love? What would a person do with that ability? What sorts of problems would it cause them? Then my husband and I went to Iceland for our honeymoon, and I was entranced by the landscape and the Viking history. So I tried putting my poor, lost love-seer into an Icelandic-flavored setting, and it clicked. Gudrun fell out of my head and onto the page, and I went with it.

A question for the author

Q: If your writing style were a bird, what type of bird would it be and why?

A: Good grief, you realize you're asking this question of a total bird nerd, right? I mean, some of my writing friends say that a story isn't one of my mine unless it has a bird in it. I share my house with parakeets, I feed the outside birds, and I have been a lifelong birdwatcher. So birds means a lot to me.

Let me think carefully about this. I write slowly, so my writing style would not be a fast hummingbird or falcon. It also wouldn't be something like a bluebird, which can have multiple broods per year. I also don't think I have a terribly flashy style, so it wouldn't be a peacock or bird of paradise. I also don't write well in crowds or coffee shops or anything like that. I'm definitely a loner writer. So my writing style wouldn't be anything that congregates in huge flocks—no flamingos or starlings or budgerigars. I also write best at home, in familiar settings, so no birds that fly long distances like terns or albatrosses.

After all of this, I think my writing style is a kakapo. What is a kakapo, you ask? A rare flightless parrot from New Zealand. They breed very slowly, with the parrots taking several years to reach maturity, and some years they don't breed at all. They have muted green feathers and aren't flashy, but have a fluffy cuteness that I find absolutely endearing. They are also loners and don't congregate in flocks like many other parrots. Because they don't fly, they stick close to home. All of these things resonate for my writing style. In addition, because they are so rare, they have a dedicated team of extraordinary scientists and volunteers who do tremendous conservation work to save the species. While I don't need conservationists for my writing, I am lucky enough to have family and writing friends who support my work, and I am very grateful to them. [On a side note, if you are so moved to learn more about kakapos, visit the Kakapo Conservation page: https://www.doc.govt.nz/our-work/kakapo-recovery/.]

About the author

Kathryn Yelinek works as a librarian in Pennsylvania. In addition to the required hobbies of reading and writing, she enjoys bird watching, star-gazing, gardening, and going to see Broadway musicals. She and her husband share their home with two adorable parakeets, whom they are actively striving to make into the most spoiled birds in the Western Hemisphere. The birds don't seem to mind. Her works have appeared in *Daily Science Fiction, Deep Magic, Metaphorosis, Andromeda Spaceways Magazine*, and *Beneath Ceaseless Skies*.

www.kathrynyelinek.com

Time and Grace

Joseph Halden

Grace Soh was going to blaze across the empty American highways faster than anyone ever had, making it from coast to coast in a matter of hours: six if everything went as planned. The faster she got to the boost site in Oakland, California, the more money she'd make.

Grace would pay damages if she was late, but she would also reap the rewards if she was early. People paid a lot to have their self-driving networks and boosters maintained, and by displacing all of that skill, society had created a need for specialists like Grace.

She put up her hand to block out the annoying Atlanta sun, and squinted to check the old watch Father had given her: 08:32.

Several cars had driven by, but thankfully there'd been no sign of any employees from the rental lot. She'd pulled over half a mile outside their fences, but people barely looked out the windows anymore, let alone into the distance, so she wouldn't be noticed.

Grace lay back and felt around the underside of the rental jet car. Her small stature allowed her to worm around until she found the network card and yanked a cable out.

Networking, she thought snidely. *As if humanity has ever used connectivity for the greater good. There's a reason it's an Internet of Things, and not people.*

She watched the network flash with error messages on one lens of her VR glasses. *Good.*

"Ms. Soh, you will not be able to contact friends or family during the trip without a network connection," the car's artificial intelligence said, echoing off densely-packed innards.

"Lucky for me, that's not a problem, Brain-box."

What friends? I've turned rejection into diamond-tipped focus, she thought. *That's why I can do things no one else bothers to think of.*

The words helped control the swirling memories of being ghosted, and press them instead into a vision of herself as a ruthlessly efficient entrepreneur. She was surging ahead, leaving everyone in the dust.

"Not even your father, Ms. Soh?"

Grace froze, wondering if the AI had a backdoor to the network. It had been a few years since she'd had official training. Blazing her own trail was a point of pride, but she also had occasional moments like now when she felt needles scratch her insides, and wondered if she'd blazed the right path.

First, though, she had to know if the AI was bluffing. "My father's dead," she lied.

"Not unless he died within the last few minutes," the AI said.

"Are you spying on me?"

"I profile all my clients."

This AI was going to be trouble. Normally a jet car's AI was just smart enough to meet a client's needs, not question things and certainly not stalk someone's online presence.

Or lack thereof. Thankfully machines couldn't judge.

The rental companies must have requested 'upgrades'.

"Wonderful."

"If we had a network connection, you might be able to reach him before he goes to bed," the AI said.

Grace imagined the AI's breath smelling like burnt engine oil as she snaked her arms past layers of crud. She wrinkled her nose and blew debris from her lips. "Stop talking about my Dad, Brain-box."

"I think it bears repeating: my name is Alvus, Ms. Soh."

The AI's boldness was making it hard to focus.

Grace pictured Father, halfway across the world in a Singaporean nursing home. In his career he'd done much of the same work she did now—repairs for the transportation grid—but had never pushed himself, had always been too relaxed to save for the future.

He'd wasted too much time on relationships, and where had those gotten him? He was just as alone as the worst curmudgeons in the nursing home. The only difference was maybe how they paid for it. The curmudgeons had hoarded their life's earnings, whereas Grace's father relied on her to support him. The end result for both was the same.

The support Grace had to send Father left little room and resources to plan her own future. Time was thereby made an even more precious commodity, and she had to rush toward her goals if she was to have any chance at realizing them.

"Ms. Soh," the AI continued in a voice from all sides, formless and lifeless. "I must inform you that what you are doing is illegal. I urge you to reconnect and disengage from any further modifications to the vehicle if you wish to avoid a flag on your file."

Grace gritted her teeth. *You think I care about a flag on my file? A tiny flag, buried in a sea of monetized data? If it means one less company trying to sell me something, then good.*

Such flags, such algorithms, made Grace want to wash her hands after engineering work. The majority of the machinery and code she worked on was beautiful—the ugliest parts most resembled humans.

She wished she could make the modifications with the AI disconnected, but several processor overrides had to be active to allow her to tinker—and the first step was to prevent the annoying AI from calling the cops. "It's a good thing you're going to forget this whole thing when our trip's over, Brain-box."

"Ms. Soh, my name is Alvus. And if you are threatening me, you should know my memory is backed up in several onboard locations, and erasure of an AI's logs is a federal offence."

You're a smart one, Grace thought for the second time. *Usually they only spout a list of specifications back at me when I suggest amnesia.*

Grace slid out from beneath the car and stood. She toggled her VR lens through different diagnostic menus, checking her work.

Half a mile away, several more cars pulled out of the fenced rental car lot, and passed Grace. A few years ago she might have hidden off the main road. But these days people blackened their windows and worked or slept as soon as they got into the self-driving cars. Grace had total faith that, here as in other areas of her life, no one would notice her.

Tumbleweeds rolled dry and crackling across the arid plain, capable of ignoring all the trivial minutiae along the route. Soon Grace would be joining them, but would be far, far faster.

She got into the cabin and opened up the dash.

"I can also be sure to notify your father of your behaviour," Alvus said after the lengthy silence.

"Keep it up, Brain-box, and you won't remember which way is up when we're done."

"I propose a trade, Ms. Soh. If you call me Alvus, I will not mention your father."

Grace uncovered the panel for the speedometer. She had to be careful not to jar any of the other densely-packed sensors, but it was hard to concentrate with the annoying AI. "*Aiyah, so ma fan.* You're a feisty one, Alvus."

"I take pride in my work."

Now that the AI—Alvus—couldn't call for help, she just had to modify the speedometer's calibration to make Alvus think they were going slower—350 instead of 500 miles per hour—and upload a fake record of their trip time for the internal log. When she'd first started she hadn't bothered to override the log, and the speeding ticket almost cost her her job. Now she knew better.

She checked and double-checked a circuit board to make sure she had the right cable. *Damn*, she thought after feeling with her fingers to count the wires for the fourth time. There was an extra one, which meant the model had changed. *Damn, damn, damn.*

Grace disconnected one of the cables and plugged her phone into the board in its place. The program would either take or it wouldn't—there was not enough time to change it. She would get much further ahead if she just tried, rather than getting lost in the changelog details. She started the recalibration app on her phone, craning her neck to keep an eye on the screen.

"Ms. Soh, you have locked me out of sensor data."

"Only for a few seconds, Alvus, I promise," she said. *I hope.*

The program finished. A few minutes later, Grace started the car. She hefted her bag into the back cabin. No time to waste securing her tools and parts—it was a short trip anyway. Another fifteen minutes saved, more money for Grace, and the closer she was to getting all she wanted.

Focus on the goal, and get there as fast as possible. Become like an Anchieta's dune lizard that dances with spiny-scaled toes so it never sinks into the sand.

"Okay, Alvus, you have the sensor data?"

"I am surprised I do, Ms. Soh. I am also surprised my path is fairly restricted, curiously correlated to your intended journey. And I'm locked out of flagging or emergency actions." Alvus let out a burst of static. "You must have done this before."

Take out the ugly, human parts, Grace thought, *and the machine becomes beautiful.*

She smiled, tapping the front display to blacken the windows. "I have no idea what you're talking about."

Grace typed away with her VR glasses on, a low hum the only evidence of the car's incredible speed. Her linked phone recorded the indirect measurements that added metadata to her workflow from implanted biometrics. She'd recorded a quick voice log as she left—a habit that had over the years become a comforting ritual, because she trusted her phone more than she trusted people when it came to her innermost thoughts. She could go back to the logs later, whenever she wanted, without having to worry about their accuracy or emotional state.

With all that data, her phone knew Grace better than she did.

"Ms. Soh, I am disoriented without accurate GPS tracking," Alvus said.

"It's good for your brain, Alvus."

"It is far more challenging to use collision-avoidance algorithms without network information. In addition to the fact that you must have modified my speed calibration, for my approach vectors need constant re-evaluation. I don't think I have ever gone this fast before. You have tied my hands."

A metaphor? Grace thought with a frown, then patted the dashboard. "It's a good thing you're up for the challenge. But I have work to do, so let me concentrate *lah!*"

She finished her report on the Atlanta boost-station repair she'd finished that morning, outlining the challenges and future upgrades necessary to push people travelling on the main trunks up to the new speed limit. Part of her knew it was a losing battle; she'd already seen the decline in federal funding for transportation lines. People had almost stopped going out when they could use VR for everything from family dinners to romantic getaways. Hell, Grace probably wouldn't go out herself if her job didn't require it.

Her work repairing recharge-boost stations would soon be obsolete, when only goods would need to be transported, and those by maglev. Her uncertain future was part of the reason she'd made a gamble on getting to site in Oakland on a tight timeline. The city was offering a lot of money to get its station back up before a weekend series of Major League Baseball games, one of a few American habits not yet lost to VR. No scheduled flights could have gotten her there in time.

The compartment rattled, and Grace's fingers typed an incoherent stream on the keyboard. "Alvus, are you having trouble?"

"Do you mean in addition to what you've already provided me?"

"Yes." She put away her keyboard, took off her glasses and opened up the instrument display on the dash. The rattling increased, and her teeth hammered together.

"I've lost connection to the lateral dampeners," Alvus said. "The engines are overheating. There—there is much cross-talk on all instrument channels."

Grace confirmed it on her own display, her pulse quickening. Her shoulders tensed and she sat up. If she'd messed something up during the speedometer recalibration... "Slow us down, turn all PCB TECs to max cooling. Clear the w—windows."

Grace gripped the leather seat next to her as she bounced up and down. Her seat harness locked with the sudden acceleration.

The shade lowered and let in blinding sunlight. "Filters, Alvus, filters!" Grace said.

"I'm losing control." His monotone voice chilled her.

"What do you mean?!"

"—can't tell what—measuring. Controls not responding." Alvus's voice clipped as the cabin heaved and rocked.

Grace's eyes adjusted to the brilliant light in time to take in the elevated highway, the brown-gold shrub plains around them, and the fact they were angled for the edge. "Alvus, turn left! Turn, turn!"

Alvus might have tried; everything happened too fast to tell. Instruments beeped as they soared over the edge of the freeway. If there had been a need for railings, they would have done little to stop the jet bullet. Polymer vibrated a drum snare. The dry wasteland surged up. Freeway pillars disappeared beyond Grace's periphery.

The landing kicked in the airbags, a white punch of mercy. The harness straps cut into Grace. Her skull shuddered. The car came to a stop, and Grace waited, breathless.

Grace turned everything off—including Alvus—then groped her way out of the car, shoving through airbags. Her skin burned from the harness; her neck ached. Smoke and hissing met her outside.

Grace stumbled through the dirt, avoiding shrubs and fist-sized rocks that had somehow not torn holes in the hull. She took in the details of the crash one by one. The car had landed nose-down in a small, dried-up ravine. The sharp front end was pushed in but intact. Ripples cascaded along the polymer skin of the main body. Smoke billowed from both of the half-meter turbines, and the right one had a small dent in it.

She pulled out her phone, a big dent in the back and spider webs of glass on the front. The screen still lit, but she had no network connection. She groaned and tucked it away.

The one-in-a-million time the connection to someone might be useful, she thought.

Grace rubbed her temples. Her watch read 12:15. She did a few mental calculations and realized she must be somewhere in New Mexico or Arizona. She was supposed to be in Oakland by 15:00. If she didn't start the work tonight, she'd be paying Oakland damages for breaking her commitment.

"Damn it." She climbed to the top of the ravine. A flat expanse stretched up to a jagged, isolated mountain visible on the edge of the horizon. Bushes and tufts of wildflowers patched the space between. Sand brushed the color from everything. The air shriveled Grace's nose. On the other side of the ravine, towering pillars of the freeway raised a dark scar in the sky.

"Any help would be great!" Grace shouted, her words drying and withering into the earth. She heard distant barks and yelps from no particular direction, formless sounds of the shrub lands.

"No answer. Of course," she muttered.

After making sure she had enough power to spare, she sat down in the front seat and turned on Alvus.

"You there?"

Alvus emitted soft warm-up audio reminiscent of a sigh. "I am, Ms. Soh."

She felt hot shame for being comforted by the way his voice mimicked a real person.

"Things are bad," she said.

But not so bad I can't get through this on my own, as I always have, she told herself.

"There is significant damage."

Grace listened to Alvus list what they had—spare turbine blades, extra cooling and lubricant, a hefty can of jet fuel, a first aid kit, a survival kit and a water tank.

Looking up toward the baking sun, Grace mouthed thanks that the water tank had survived. She didn't know how long she might last in the heat otherwise.

Then Alvus spouted a stream of everything that had malfunctioned, and would need manual inspection: all instruments, voltage lines, thermoelectric cooler drivers…

"Alvus," she murmured, "do you know much about the X2 line of cars before you?"

"I have extensive knowledge for marketing purposes."

Grace rolled her eyes. "Of course you do." She sank against the seat. Part of her didn't want to ask, didn't want to reveal how stupid she may have been. At this point there was a least a sliver of doubt it wasn't her fault. She let the words scrape out. "Were the voltage levels on the instrument card changed?"

"Yes, Ms. Soh. They were dropped from six to three-point-three volts for power consumption."

Oh God. How many chips did I fry? Grace blew out air.

Looking in the back cabin, it only took Grace a moment to realize the debris and bits were all that was left of the transponder and emergency beacon. They'd been smashed by her rugged tools bouncing around in the back. *Why didn't I secure my crap?*

Grace got out and buried her face in the crook of her elbow. She couldn't call for help. She was alone, and she hated herself for letting it make her feel so weak.

The time: 17:00. Grace had crossed the threshold from bonus to penalties, and every minute that went by put more distance between her and profit.

The jet car's long shadows stretched across the ravine, pre-cursing the coming darkness. The pools of sweat beneath Grace's arms had grown sticky and itchy. She took a swig of water from her bottle, and wiped her brow.

In a nearby section of the ravine where the slope steepened from aggressive erosion, tumbleweeds had gathered, caught and shuddering from the wind that could no longer push them. It seemed Grace wasn't the only one whose travel plans had been cut short.

She sighed and ducked back into the turbine. She'd heard barks and yelps in the distance throughout the day, and they grew louder and more frequent as the sun dipped.

She'd found work-arounds for burnt chips on three circuit boards, working with Alvus to find alternative modes of operation.

He was actually being very helpful. Machines were always much more reliable than people.

She cleaned debris and tested the boards—they showed basic functionality, but she had to admit she was out of her depth and was just lucky she'd had her soldering iron with her for the service trip. And that they had energy to spare.

"Can you connect to the turbines now, Alvus?" She backed away and listened for the hum of charge. "Come on," she muttered, clasping her hands together.

After a lengthy silence, a howl echoed across the plain, as though the wild had somehow triumphed over her efforts.

Are those coyotes, or wolves? Grace groaned. *I don't need this right now.*

She threw her arms against the turbine. The bang echoed between the shadows of the shrubs.

"I am sorry, Ms. Soh."

Grace sank with her back against the car, lowering herself into the shade.

Her lips trembled, and she wrestled within herself for the instinctive favour she wanted to ask of a machine.

To make it seem more human. God, she was pathetic.

Grace, you've gotta get through this, one way or another, she thought. *Got enough on your plate. We'll sort out that other crap later.*

"Call me Grace, Alvus," she said at last. "We're going to be spending a lot more time together."

As if that were the only reason. As if her creeping desperation weren't making her take solace in an artificial construct.

She snatched her water bottle and drank. Thank god the car's water tank was intact. She let a few streams dribble down her cheeks and onto her shirt. A few hours ago it had been cool. Now it burned on its way down.

The feeling reminded her of a thousand coffees, all sipped alone, at restaurants and cafes where others met friends.

There's no one I could call, she thought, *even if I had a network connection.*

She swallowed hard and put the bottle's cap back on.

None of that matters, Grace, she told herself. *Get a grip.*

She froze.

A coyote stood watching her from fifteen feet away. When she caught its eye, it looked down, feigning interest in a patch of dead wildflowers. Its sand-colored pelt was spotted with flecks and patches of black and white.

The coyote kept sneaking glances at her, trotting in a radius around her. It was bigger than a German Shepherd.

Oh God. That's no coyote—that's a coywolf.

The coywolf's long tail—more full and fluffy than the rest of its body—nearly touched the ground behind its legs. The tail wagged absently but halted every time the coywolf stopped to steal a glance at Grace. Bands of black fur highlighted an intensity behind its eyes.

The waterfalls of sweat down her sides suddenly chilled. She'd heard stories of the coywolves changing, migrating to unexpected areas, looting and eating just about anything they could find, destroying equipment and animals indiscriminately as resources grew more scarce. She raised herself and clenched her hands to stop them from trembling.

She charged forward. "Go on! Get out of here!"

The coywolf darted back, then bent low to the ground and snarled.

Grace's calves ached from the sudden burst, and she had the sense of settling into a new normal for slow reaction time.

Not good, Grace. Not good.

"Get going! There's nothing for you here!"

She ran after the coywolf. The creature locked eyes now, running half-backward, able to maintain that posture with Grace's stumbling lope. She continued after it until her legs wouldn't anymore. She growled as she bent down to pick up a few pebbles to throw at the coywolf.

She walked backward all the way back to the jet car. The coywolf stayed where it was, watching her the whole way.

"Grace, are you all right?" Alvus had turned on loud external speakers.

"I don't know, Alvus," she said.

"You don't appear to have any additional injuries."

"Glad to know you've got your eye on me."

"Many eyes."

Grace held up a hand, and opened the door to the car. "That's enough, creepo, thanks." She bent the seat back so she could lie down.

"Grace, you've made excellent progress," Alvus said. "There is still work to be done, and I recommend trying to get out before nightfall."

Grace shook her head, squeezing her eyes shut. "I haven't made good progress," she whispered. "I've lost thousands of dollars since I've been stuck here."

The sun had lowered to cast the whole ravine in shadow now, and the dry whispers taunted Grace with all she'd gotten wrong. All her failures. Inadequacies.

She reached up and slammed the car door shut.

"Grace, I am sure you can recover the lost wages," Alvus said, his volume adjusting to her tone.

Even with the door closed, she couldn't stop the voice inside chiding her for pretending, more and more with each minute that passed, that Alvus was a person.

So pathetic.

"Probably," she muttered. She wanted to ask why she still felt so awful, but her inner critic's mocks grew louder, silencing her.

The time: 21:00. Strands of sunlight dangled like outstretched arms as the horizon pulled away. Several more tumbleweeds had gotten caught in the pile in the ravine, rattling against each other like a pile of bones.

Grace slid back beneath the jet car, her head aching from trying to wade through the never-ending series of repairs. Every shortcut she'd made before the trip had added more repair work, a thousand tiny wounds bleeding out any hope of getting ahead. She'd cut the feathers off the bird to make it fly faster.

She puzzled over the thermoelectric cooling circuitry, trying to get some temperature control back to key current drivers. Her phone light was a poor substitute for ambient light, and she kept having to twist around in the cramped space.

"How's that? What's the temperature, Alvus?"

"Twenty-nine point-four degrees Celsius."

Grace sighed. "Okay. Try turning on the cooler now."

She bumped her head on the way out, making the world spin as she wiggled out from beneath the car. She rested against the side for a moment, then pawed her way around the turbine to the back for some water.

A few steps away a coywolf lapped at a puddle of water dribbling from the water tank. Another one craned its neck above and gnawed at a water hose.

"Hey!" Grace shouted.

The one licking the puddle looked up, yellow eyes meeting hers. It growled, its lips quaking spittle.

Grace yelled and stomped the ground. "Get going! Get!"

The coywolf snapped its jaws.

A bear's roar from the car shook the surrounding shrubs. The coywolves jumped and the one let go of the water line.

Grace charged the pair of coywolves with her arms raised as Alvus continued to roar from the speakers. The sound made her teeth rattle. She tried to kick one, and it bit her shoe. She careened against the side of the car. She swung her phone's light in the coywolf's eyes, and it released.

The other coywolf pushed onto its back heels then dove at her. She jumped and landed on its paw. It yipped; others answered in the distance.

Grace backed up, and leapt inside the car.

Despite Alvus's attempts to ward them off with loud noises, the coywolves quickly realized he posed no real threat. They started worming their noses back into every open crevice of the half-repaired jet car.

They were going to tear the car apart if she didn't do something.

Grace scrambled through the survival kit in the back cabin, darting glances up at the coywolves. *Come on, give me something.*

The coywolf was back gnawing on the water line.

Grace found a flare gun; it almost shook out of her hands as she opened the car door.

"Leave me alone!" she shouted, taking aim.

She fired the flare gun, a popping hiss planting in the dirt right beside the coywolf clutching the water line. It jumped back growling.

"Stop taking things from me!" she went on, reloading and firing again.

This time she narrowly missed the coywolf. It yipped and fled into the darkness.

"You never help me!" she shouted. "No, we couldn't have that, now could we?"

Grace fired several more flares around the car, bathing it in red light. On the seventh one, the wind caught the flare and pulled it into the pile of blocked tumbleweeds.

It lit up like a rocket blast. Dry crackles turned quickly into a roar, and spread a hotter-than-day sun into the surrounding area. The smoke tasted hot, sharp, and empty.

Grace cringed away from the heat. She knew she should be grateful, for the fire should keep the coywolves away, but she felt an inexplicable loss at the trapped tumbleweeds' promise of a new life going up in flames. Like they'd skimmed across the steppes only to be betrayed by the force that carried them.

She watched the flames lick the sky and slowly die down. Though everything here was dry, it was too sparse to have a brush fire, thank goodness.

Grace turned back to the water tank. The water spilled out of the broken tube in thick spurts, muddying the earth.

"No, no, no!" She rushed over and tried to plug it with her hands, then a piece of her shirt. It took several minutes before she plugged the leak with first-aid tape.

She was soaked and the seal still dripped water. She shone her light in. There was maybe half a gallon left.

Grace gathered her hair in her hands and pulled.

"Why didn't you say something?" she shouted. "Alvus!"

"I didn't see the coywolves on my cameras, Grace."

"Oh, come on! You watch me with all your sensors and you just happen to flake when coywolves take all my water?" She stood and slammed the hood of the car.

"I admit my attention was occupied while we were trying to find workarounds. But my sensors didn't find any visible approach."

"I thought your processing power was better than that, Brain-box." She kicked the curved front and glared into the darkness, praying the coywolves wouldn't return.

"It is possible I am damaged in a way I cannot perceive, Grace. I am sorry."

"No you're not," Grace snapped, turning back to the car. "You don't need water. You know you'll eventually be found, and you have all the time in the world. There's nothing at stake for you—and whether I live or die doesn't matter. There's more humanity in you than I thought."

The wind snaked between leaves, chattering, whispering. The hunk of metal in the ravine remained unmoved. The tumbleweed fire was now a pile of faint embers.

"I wish I could convince you that's not the case. I only have words. I wish to help you survive this."

Grace's eyes and chest burned. She dropped her chin.

What am I doing? Chastising a machine for doing what it's been programmed to do? Come on, Grace.

She trudged back toward the front of the car. She felt heavy, burdened with an increasing list of problems she couldn't fix. Feeling pathetic for her gratitude that Alvus, despite everything she'd shouted, was here with her.

She slid under the car. "Let's keep going," she said, her voice thick.

The engine smelled of pungent lead solder, burnt oil, and ash as Grace worked on into the night.

The time: 02:00, the next morning, still dark. The howls grew louder. Grace wondered if coywolves ever slept, or if they existed just to torment her. She squinted into the night, trying to spot their slinking forms, but couldn't. She wished she were taller—then the coywolves might be more afraid.

She shone a light on her blackened hands, trying to rub the oil off without success. The taste of smoke from the tumbleweed fire still lingered in her throat. "Alvus, what do you know about lateral stabilization chips?"

"I am not authorized to share that information, Grace. I'm locked out for safety reasons, to prevent exactly what you're suggesting."

Grace groaned. Of course. Because humans are so endlessly stupid, herself included.

She was so tired, thirsty and hungry. She was trying to stretch the water out but it was difficult when she exerted herself so much. The tank had been leaking so much it had been pointless to try and make the water last.

She thought the lateral stabilization was the last step. They seemed achingly close to a working car, but she didn't trust herself at all anymore.

"There's got to be a way," she said. "A loophole in your programming."

Alvus hummed—something he'd never done before.

"Uh—are you okay?"

"I suggest you look at the maintenance logs," Alvus said abruptly.

"What do you mean?" Grace asked. "What will I find there?"

"I do not know. It is an option." The screen inside lit up with a crude, pixelated, winking eye.

Does an AI know when it's losing its mind? she wondered before she sat down in front. She kept the door open in case she had to bolt for it. It did little to ease the knot in her stomach.

If Alvus had given out on her, there was nowhere she could go. She could try to climb the pillars of the freeway, and hope someone happened to notice her as they passed at subsonic speeds.

But they wouldn't, and she would be even more alone.

She tapped the screen and scanned the logs. She found several hundred entries for oil changes, a few for turbine changes, then—

"You're smarter than you look, Alvus."

"My current appearance is entirely your fault, Grace."

She almost laughed. "Okay. I deserved that. So there was a log two years ago where the lateral stabilization chip had a firmware upgrade, and some manual calibration done. Can you show me your records from that log?"

"No. You do not have authorization."

Grace smacked the dash. "Come on! Are you just messing with me now? Why even bother showing me then?"

"I thought it might spark some ideas. I am not authorized to say more."

If I ever get out of this, I will hunt down the vehicle safety manager and lock him in a suicide cruise-control trip straight into the Pacific.

A few bursts of static sprayed out the speakers, then another crudely pixelated image appeared on the screen. This time it spelled a message in barely recognizable lettering: "Enter my mind."

Realization wormed icy fingers around Grace's core. *That's what he's hinting at. Interface with his consciousness, and piece through his recordings.*

To do that, she'd have to connect through her phone, which recorded

everything about her, not to mention all
the personal logs she'd made. If she let
Alvus in, then he would see how many
times she'd rigged other jet cars to travel
illegally fast across the country.

He'd also see deeper—much deeper.
His inquiries into the health of her father
were a handshake by comparison. What
would Alvus do with all that information?
Machines weren't supposed to be capable
of judgment, but throughout this whole
ordeal, Alvus had shown many more signs
of humanity than any other AI she'd
known.

Hell, more than some of the friends
she'd once had.

She was both grateful and ashamed,
especially now that she worried about the
possibility of his judgment. If he was
showing so many other signs of humanity,
was he just as capable of looking at her
bared soul, and rejecting her?

She stared at the phone clutched in
her hand. If only she could delete or lock
Alvus out of the many years of logs and
personal metadata, but those were deeply
entwined with the algorithms that
protected her mind in the rare cases when
activities like mentally soaring through
reams of data were necessary.

Was this the only way? Risk everything in a total admission of her inner self, or be eaten by coywolves?

Or maybe she'd end up just like the tumbleweeds, sailing straight into cremation.

"Grace," Alvus said, "are you all right?"

Coywolves barked, very close.

It was this or die. Grace put on her VR glasses, hooked up her phone, and jacked in.

She blazed past red walls and skirted encryption barriers, typing away furiously. As she crossed the threshold, she sensed Alvus now had complete access to her digital presence.

Don't judge me, Alvus.

Shuddering, she moved into Alvus's recordings.

Please don't abandon me.

Men and women slept in car seats, worked, careened along in typical journeys, the windows always blackened. Grace skipped through these until she saw a suited woman walking ahead of the car, a rocky knoll ahead. The woman took one last look at the camera, then walked off the cliff.

Mortified, Grace traced the woman's other recordings, trying to make some sense of what she'd seen. It seemed the woman's company had arranged a long-term lease that meant she was using Alvus all the time.

The woman's history followed a similar pattern to Grace's own life, commuting daily from New York to Seattle, working the entire way. Alvus attempted to cheer her up. The woman never responded to him. The bags beneath her eyes grew heavier, the life leaking out and leaving a deadness in her stare.

The woman didn't seem there when she killed herself. She had been vacant, leeched of something ineffable.

There wasn't a single piece of evidence of the woman talking to another human being. Grace went back and forth through the footage, seeing more and more resonance of the woman's life with her own. Her temperature rose as her mind went into overdrive. She felt at any moment now the heat could set her ablaze.

It didn't have to end this way, she kept telling the woman. *You could have called someone. You could have called me.*

Even as she thought the words, the absurd impossibility stared her in the face.

Was she on the road to becoming that woman?

Even worse, was she already there?

Keep going, Grace, just keep going.

But she'd been racing... for so very long. Just as the woman had. What was the point of it all, if it ended the same way?

She mentally flipped through the logs, back and forth, back and forth, until she felt herself drifting deeper into a whirlpool.

The view jolted and was replaced by recordings made out the side and back cameras. They were of sunsets and sunrises, brilliant gold, flamingo, and lilac layers as the sun bid hello or goodbye.

This wasn't a required recording; this was something Alvus chose to do.

He was trying to help her.

He cared.

With great effort, Grace pulled herself back and navigated through more of the regular recordings.

She finally found recordings of the maintenance engineer putting in a new chip. She had to cross-link to the firmware changes, and the manual calibration gave her the encryption keys. She copied the encryption algorithms, checked them, then pulled out, backing through the firewalls.

She felt raw.

She breathed heavily, words emerging in slow chunks. "Alvus, I have them," she said. "Can you copy them into one of your processors?"

"I suggest the interface module," he said. "If you short wires from the J1 header, that should give me control."

Grace glanced out the back of the car toward the towering rock. A mile away the ground writhed with movement. The coywolves had brought reinforcements, and would devour the exposed parts of the car if she didn't act soon. Her heart leapt into her throat.

She lurched out and slid beneath the car. Her soldering iron sat plugged into a battery, a mess of wires and solder beside. Grace grabbed the wires and got to work.

"Grace," Alvus said, "a pack of—"

"Thanks, I saw." She fought to still her shaking hands. Flecks of solder flew off and burned her cheeks.

"Grace, they're almost here."

Yips and barks answered.

She had four of five wires done when a coywolf bit her shoe. It tugged, shook until her shoe came off, then retreated, gnashing, and tearing. It was only a matter of time until the shoe wasn't enough.

She got the last wire on, but there was too much solder. It had shorted a few of the pins. She jabbed with the soldering iron, trying to drag off some of the excess. Once, twice—there.

"Alvus," she cried, "start the turbines! Please! Start the tur—"

The roar drowned out the howls and the yips.

Grace screamed joyfully and almost embraced the rumbling engine. She slid out and into the front seat.

"Alvus, let's go!"

The jet car surged backward out of the ravine. On-ramps were rare, but by going slowly and carefully across the plains, she and Alvus would eventually find one. Grace had never been so happy to be in a moving vehicle.

The time: 06:15. Grace walked out of the booster station, still missing her shoe, and opened the car door. "Hi, Alvus."

"Hello, Grace. Are you feeling better?"

"A little bit," she said, sinking into the seat. "I got the station working again."

"And the payment?"

She sighed. "Well, I don't have to pay them too much for being late. Didn't make anything, though."

"I am sorry, Grace."

"It's all right." She meant the words, and just felt glad the whole thing was over. She valued the time ahead to breathe at her own pace, surprising herself. She had never expected to want a vacation after a lifetime seeing Father waste so much time.

Then again, she was finding more and more that maybe her expectations needed recalibration.

She paused, then: "I also spoke to my Dad. It felt good." Another unexpected outcome—that she'd end up acting on and agreeing with an AI's advice. As well as reaching out to another human being.

"I'm very glad to hear that."

She hesitated, thinking back to their shared time in digital space. "When you and I connected, I…"

Alvus's voice shifted in tone, almost imperceptibly. Grace wouldn't have noticed had she not spent almost an entire day with him. "I am grateful for the glimpse into you, Grace," he said, his vocal cadence slower. "I will not disrespect that trust."

"You don't… think less of me now? That I'm just, I don't know, not worth the effort?" she whispered. The words burned her. A day before she wouldn't have given them voice, wouldn't have allowed herself to sink this low. But she had to confirm if the glimpse inside had revealed what had turned so many others away.

"No, Grace. Humans are remarkable in their ability to break the chain of what has come before—something I cannot do. Something I wish I could do."

Grace ran her hands through her hair.

She'd gone from coast to coast, and still she had so far to go.

"Thank you, Alvus," she said.

"Thank you for not wiping my brain-box."

Grace rubbed her forehead, remembering that she still had to return

Alvus, which would involve paying a lot for damage. Alvus's memory would also be wiped somewhat to protect privacy, though maybe he'd found a way around that with some of his recordings. For the first time, she wondered what a memory wipe must feel like to an AI.

The next words came out of her unwittingly. "Alvus, how much would your company charge for your purchase?"

Alvus paused before replying. "Are you wanting to keep me around, Grace?"

"How would you… feel about that?"

"As terrific as I am capable."

"So how much?"

Alvus quoted a figure. It was far more than Grace had expected—much more than the damage costs would be—and would use up most of her savings. But maybe it was a worthwhile investment.

Nearby, a tumbleweed was stuck against a signpost at the edge of the boost station. Grace couldn't help herself. She walked over, picked it up carefully, looking around for where the wind would take it, then moved half a mile up the road to set it down where it had the best chances of a long journey.

Her mind kept wanting to surge ahead, to plan the next project, but for the first time in a long while, she told herself *No*. Maybe it was okay to pause along the way.

By the time she returned to Alvus, the sun had crept up closer to the silver line of the horizon. "Do you want to turn to face the sunrise?" Grace asked gently.

"Thank you, but no. I've recorded many of them."

Grace frowned. She stared at the orange-crimson fingers ushering in the new day—she never thought she'd seen anything more moving.

She knew it felt this way, in part, because Alvus was here with her. Maybe that was okay, too.

"What I do want," Alvus continued, "is to hear how you see it with your eyes."

See Joseph Halden's story "Time and Grace" online at Metaphorosis.
If you liked it, leave a comment. Authors love that!
Remember to subscribe to our e-mail updates so you'll know when new stories are posted.

About the story

I'm always interested in our relationship with technology, and the specific ways it influences our connections to each other. The specific idea for this story, however, was planted when I was travelling for work, in a new rental vehicle every time. It was a lonely period of my life. I was in grad school and commuting to different experiments, in places where I hardly knew anyone. The scenery and places that I visited in and around California's bay area were spectacular. Although I tried to enjoy the ride, it was hard to have no one to share it with.

Throughout my trips I mused about people's relationships with their vehicles, as well as how vehicles are becoming increasingly intelligent. They become comforting homes, a familiar refuge when everything around us changes. Listening to familiar songs, even sitting in a familiar seat, can be very calming when there are few constants. I started to imagine a road trip with an artificial intelligence to keep a person company, and if that might be one area of people's lives where artificial intelligence might be more welcome than others, because of the strong person-vehicle relationship that exists within the North American cultural mythos. These ideas all came before home assistants, or even voice commands on smartphones.

Road trips have a certain mystique about them, but as notions of self-driving cars began permeating the technological landscape, I realized my original vision of a more traditional North American road trip might not be something that would even exist once we had artificial intelligences in cars. I needed to come up with a scheme where someone on a trip would be forced to consider their surroundings, rather than tune out and wait to reach their destination.

I wanted to explore some of the loss that can be engendered by new technology, and I thus created Grace Soh, one of a select few who still used the rapid highways, and who most pointedly felt such a loss. In our technophilic society, it can be very easy to adopt new creations without being mindful of what we might be transformed as a result. Grace embodies that tendency to race ahead without paying attention.

The rest is... well, in the story's veins. I have to thank Mary Robinette Kowal for her great initial feedback on the story during the Odyssey Writing Workshop, as well as many others who helped shape the story into what it is.

Oh, one more fun fact: I use Alvus as a persona in many stories where I have an AI, and I'm thrilled he fit so well into this one.

A question for the author

Q: What is the most recent book that you lost sleep reading/thinking about?

A: I adored *Among Others* by Jo Walton, and couldn't stop reading. The depiction of magic in such an unfathomable yet human way was mesmerizing. The protagonist's journey held so many beautifully-articulated moments of humanity that really worked for me, and I loved re-experiencing some sci-fi classics through her lens.

About the author

Joseph Halden is a wizard in search of magic, an astronaut in need of space, and a hopeless enthusiast of frivolity. He's shot things with giant lasers, worn an astronaut costume for over 100 days to try and get into space, and made his own soap. A graduate of the Odyssey Writing Workshop, he writes science fiction and fantasy in the Canadian prairies.

www.josephhalden.com, @joseph_halden

Copyright

Title information

Metaphorosis June 2020

ISSN: 2573-136X (online)
ISBN: 978-1-64076-171-1 (e-book)
ISBN: 978-1-64076-172-8 (paperback)

Copyright

Publisher

Metaphorosis
a magazine of speculative fiction

Metaphorosis Magazine is an imprint of Metaphorosis Publishing
Neskowin, OR, USA

Discounts available

Substantial discounts are available for educational institutions, including writing workshops. Discounts are also available for quantity purchases. For details, contact Metaphorosis at metaphorosis.com/about

Metaphorosis Publishing

Metaphorosis offers beautifully written science fiction and fantasy. Our imprints include:

Metaphorosis Magazine
Plant Based Press
Verdage

You can also find us:
@MetaphorosisMag, @MetaphorosisRev, @Metaphorosis
www.facebook.com/metaphorosis

Help keep Metaphorosis running by supporting us at
Patreon.com/metaphorosis

See more about some of our books on the following pages.

Metaphorosis
a magazine of speculative fiction

Metaphorosis is an online speculative fiction magazine dedicated to quality writing. We publish an original story every week, along with author bios, interviews, and notes on story origins.

We also publish monthly print and e-book issues, as well as yearly Best of and Complete anthologies.

Come and see us online at magazine.Metaphorosis.com

Metaphorosis:
Best of 2019

The best science
fiction and fantasy
stories from
Metaphorosis
magazine's fourth
year.

Metaphorosis
2019

All the stories
from *Metaphorosis*
magazine's fourth
year. Fifty-two
great SFF stories.

Metaphorosis: Best of 2018

The best science fiction and fantasy stories from *Metaphorosis* magazine's third year.

Metaphorosis 2018

All the stories from *Metaphorosis* magazine's third year. Fifty-two great SFF stories.

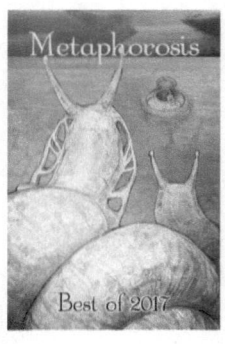 

Metaphorosis: Best of 2017

The best science fiction and fantasy stories from *Metaphorosis* magazine's *second* year.

Metaphorosis 2017

All the stories from *Metaphorosis* magazine's second year. Fifty-three great SFF stories.

Metaphorosis:
Best of 2016

The best science
fiction and fantasy
stories from
Metaphorosis
magazine's first
year.

Metaphorosis
2016

Almost all the
stories from
Metaphorosis
magazine's first
year.

Plant Based Press

plant
based
press

Vegan-friendly science fiction and fantasy, including an annual anthology of the year's best SFF stories.

Best Vegan SFF of 2019

The best vegan-friendly science fiction and fantasy stories of 2019!

Best Vegan SFF of 2018

The best vegan-friendly science fiction and fantasy stories of 2018!

Best Vegan SFF of 2017

The best vegan-friendly science fiction and fantasy stories of 2017!

Best Vegan SFF of 2016

The best vegan-friendly science fiction and fantasy stories of 2016!

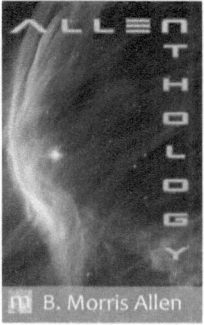

Susurrus

A darkly romantic story of magic, love, and suffering.

Allenthology: Volume I

A quarter century of SFF, including the full contents of the collections *Tocsin, Start with Stones,* and *Metaphorosis.*

Verdage

Science fiction and fantasy books for writers – full of great stories, often with an additional focus on the craft of speculative fiction writing.

Score

an SFF symphony

What if stories were written like music? *Score* is an anthology of varied stories arranged to follow an emotional score from the heights of joy to the depths of despair – but always with a little hope shining through.

Reading 5X5

Five stories, five times

Twenty-five SFF authors, five base stories, five versions of each – see how different writers take on the same material, with stories in contemporary and high fantasy, soft and hard SF, and a mysterious 'other' category.

Reading 5X5

Writers' Edition

All the stories from the regular, readers' edition, plus two extra stories, the story seed, and authors' notes on writing. Over 100 pages of additional material specifically aimed at writers.